YOU'RE INVITED

DON'T MISS THESE OTHER GREAT
BOOKS BY THESE AUTHORS

BY JEN MALONE
At Your Service

BY GAIL NALL
Breaking the Ice

YOU'RE INVITED

BY JEN MALONE &
GAIL NALL

ALADDIN M!X
NEW YORK LONDON TORONTO SYDNEY NEW DELHI

ALADDIN M!X

Simon & Schuster Children's Publishing Division

1230 Avenue of the Americas, New York, New York 10020

This Aladdin M!X edition May 2015

Text copyright © 2015 by Jennifer Malone and Gail Nall

Cover illustration copyright © 2015 by Marilena Perilli

Also available in an Aladdin hardcover edition.

For information about special discounts for bulk purchases, please contact

Simon & Schuster Special Sales at 1-866-506-1949 or business@simonandschuster.com.

The Simon & Schuster Speakers Bureau can bring authors to your live event. For more information or to book an event contact the Simon & Schuster Speakers Bureau at 1-866-248-3049 or visit our website at www.simonspeakers.com.

Book design by Laura Lyn DiSiena

The text of this book was set in Bembo.

Manufactured in the United States of America 0415 OFF

10 9 8 7 6 5 4 3 2 1

Library of Congress Cataloging-in-Publication Data

Malone, Jen, author.

You're invited / by Jen Malone and Gail Nall.

p. cm.

Summary: When twelve-year-old Sadie is fired from her mother's wedding planning company after a disastrous mishap, she starts her own party planning business and recruits her three best friends.

[1. Parties—Fiction. 2. Birthdays—Fiction. 3. Business enterprises—Fiction. 4. Best friends—Fiction. 5. Friendship—Fiction. 6. Beaches—Fiction.] I. Nall, Gail, author.

II. Title. III. Title: R.S.V.P.

PZ7.M29642Yo 2015   [Fic]—dc23   2014031625

ISBN 978-1-4814-3197-2 (hc)

ISBN 978-1-4814-3196-5 (pbk)

ISBN 978-1-4814-3198-9 (eBook)

TO MOM AND DAD,
FOR SUMMERS IN OCEAN PARK
AND SO MUCH MORE
—J. M.

TO EVA,
WHO LOVES THE SAND AND THE WAVES
—G. N.

UNDER THE SEA

Mr. and Mrs. Patrick and Leslie Westfall

together with

Ms. Stephanie Jordan

invite you to be "Part of Our World" at the wedding

of our (mer)children

Cassidy and Christopher

on Saturday, June 20,

at five o'clock.

Chris will "Kiss the Girl" aboard the Windward Eclipse,

Slip seventeen at Sandpiper Beach Marina,

1004 Sandpiper Drive, Sandpiper Beach, North Carolina

Dress: Seaside Formal, "Tails" optional

Reception immediately following

RSVP to Lorelei Pleffer of Pleffer's Picture-Perfect Weddings

at (910) 555-0192, by June 5

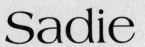

Sadie

TODAY'S TO-DO LIST:
- ☐ sync watch with Mom's
- ☐ buy seasick medicine
- ☐ pack backup bridesmaid dresses

When I peer over the boat railing, it's not like I actually expect mermaids and mermen to be bobbing in the ocean below me. Buuuuuut then again, I wouldn't put anything past my mom. If her client wants a *Little Mermaid* wedding, her client gets a *Little Mermaid* wedding, no detail spared.

My pocket buzzes and I slide my phone out.

Plz check on photog. Thx.

I weave my way through the rows of chairs sliding back and forth on the deck. The one thing Mom doesn't control on wedding days is the weather, and today isn't exactly offering ideal sailing conditions. I hope the bride has less wobbly legs than Ariel.

"Excuse me, sir, um, are you okay?" I ask a man hanging over the boat's side.

The three cameras hanging from his neck smack against his back as he straightens. Uh-oh. He does *not* look so hot. He mumbles something under his breath and I shake my head.

"Sorry. I didn't catch that. Would you mind repeating?" I ask, using my most polite voice. Mom's trained me well.

He stares at me for a second, then screams, "I SAID I'M A LITTLE SEASICK!"

Okay, so "please repeat" does not mean "scream at your highest possible volume," but I'm kind of used to the vendors treating me differently. They think just because I'm only twelve, I'm not capable of the same things a normal wedding coordinator's assistant is.

They would be wrong.

I plant my feet hip-width apart for balance and get straight to business. "I have a seasick bracelet you can wear on your wrist, and if you give me five minutes, I can grab some of the motion-sickness medicine I packed in my emergency kit. I also have a little sister who's a pretty decent photographer, if you're okay with her using one of your cameras. She could stand at the railing and grab the shots of the bride arriving by dinghy while you wait for the medicine to kick in."

His face was already turning green when I mentioned the dinghy, but he adds a look of horror to that. "I can't allow a *child* to photograph this wedding!"

I consider telling him kids can do *lots* of stuff every bit as well as any grown-up, but then the boat rolls over a large swell, and with the way he clutches at his stomach, I don't have the heart.

Between sucking in big breaths of fresh air, he says, "My assistant will take all the important shots of the bridal party. Tell your sister she can help by getting photos of the guests."

And just like that Izzy lands herself an assignment. Ick. She'll be totally annoying and gloaty about this all week now.

But the client comes first, and my job is to save the day. Good thing I really love my job, and even more important, good thing I'm really excellent at my job, even if certain people (cough, *Mom*, cough) hardly bother to acknowledge it.

Half the time she doesn't even know I'm solving a crisis, like making sure the waiter knows the groom's grandmother is allergic to wheat or scuffing up the waxed dance floor before anyone has an epic wipeout. My job is to keep things off *her* plate, and that's what I do. Always.

My phone buzzes again. On wedding days, no one besides Mom would dare text me.

Sure enough:

All handled w/photog? Bride arrival in 6 min.

Not five minutes. Not ten minutes. *Six* minutes. And you could set your clock by Mom's schedule, too. I tell the photographer I'll be right back and race below-decks to the staging area where all the various wedding paraphernalia is located, alongside my sister, Isabelle. She's sitting on top of the backup wedding gown with her face stuck in a book.

"Izzy, you're gonna get that completely wrinkled! The bride is gonna need to wear that if she gets something on her real dress."

"Relax, Sadie. You know Mom would never let anything happen to the actual dress."

"Well, what if . . . what if a wave crashes into the dinghy on the bride's way out to the boat? How do you think Mom's gonna prevent that?"

"Umbrellas." Izzy points out the tiny round window of the cabin at a wooden dinghy motoring toward us. It's too far to make out faces, but there are definitely umbrellas bobbing along either side of one of the figures. Mom thinks of ev-er-y-thing.

I scramble back from the window and pull my sister to her feet. "Hurry up! The photographer's sick and his assistant needs your help getting shots."

Izzy squeals with excitement and follows me up the stairs. She's practically bouncing by the time we reach him. I think getting her to stop is the main reason he hands off what is probably a ridiculously expensive camera to a ten-year-old so quickly. His other hand reaches for the Dramamine and the seasick band I hold out.

He swallows the pill and then takes my advice to focus on the horizon. You don't grow up in Sandpiper Beach, North Carolina, without learning the best ways to get your sea legs.

"Izzy, head over to where the guests are and grab some shots of them watching the bridal party arrive," I instruct.

She answers with a "You're not the boss of me," but at least she does what I ask as I run to make sure the groom is in place. My favorite thing about weddings is also my least favorite: everything happens at once.

But this one is a success so far. Okay, so maybe the wedding party has a hard time getting out of their dinghies since their bridesmaid dresses have sewn-on mermaid tails, and it's true that the photographer throws up the Dramamine before it can even reach his stomach. But you can tell the bride and groom are really in love, what with the way he makes googly eyes at her as she comes down the aisle to a steel-drum version of "Kiss the Girl."

Mom slides into place beside me.

"Thanks for your help today," she whispers while giving me a squeeze around my waist.

Now it's my turn to glow. Ever since Dad died and Mom started her wedding-planning company, she's been totally preoccupied with her business. I get the whole I-need-a-distraction-from-the-grief thing, but it's almost like she wants a distraction from me and Izzy, too. So the times when she actually notices me, it's like . . . magic. Like it used to be.

I don't have that much time to savor the feeling,

though, because I need to get going on my next task. As the couple exchanges vows, I sneak belowdecks and creep over to the cage of the shaggy sheepdog who belongs to one of the bridesmaids and just *happens* to match the one in *The Little Mermaid*. I mean, what are the odds?

"You ready for your big entrance, Fake Max?" I ask, checking his collar to make sure the pouch containing the wedding rings is fastened securely around the buckle. I don't know what this dog's name is, but I've watched *The Little Mermaid* alongside my note-taking Mom enough over the past few months to know Prince Eric's dog is named Max, so it will have to do.

He woofs at me and plants a sloppy kiss on my cheek. Ick. This job has a ton of occupational hazards, and now I can add dog slobber to the list. I secure his leash and lead him above, sneaking him around the back of the seated wedding guests.

The minister smiles at the happy couple and asks, "Do you have the rings?"

That's my cue.

And then . . . it happens.

A big plop of seagull doo-doo drops from the sky and lands directly on my head, dribbling greenish-yellowish-whitish goop down my cheek. When I scream, everyone swivels as one to face me. I freeze, horrified by both my interruption and the super-slimy, super-gross stuff sliding down toward my neck.

The groom drops the bride's hands.

I drop the dog's leash.

Fake Max goes tearing off in wild circles around the deck, barking like crazy at the circling seagull, who looks like he's lining up target practice with the top of my head again.

"Grab him!" Mom screams as Fake Max pulls up at my ankles, panting hard. But I don't grab him, because:

1) I can't take my eyes from the seagull, who looks suspiciously like he's about to dive-bomb straight for my head, and

2) I'm thinking about how I'm going to use a printed program to remove bird poop from my hair.

Fake Max is eyeing the gull too, and when the bird swoops low, the dog jumps into the air at him. Of course he misses, since his shaggy fur is probably completely covering his eyes. Landing, he then tears off across the deck in hot pursuit of the bird, who I would swear is laughing more than screeching. Fake Max runs, pauses, and then jumps, chasing the seagull straight off the back of the boat, his four furry legs still running through the air, as he drops to the water below.

His owner shrieks, "SHEP!" and shuffle-runs across the deck in her mermaid dress. She doesn't even hesitate at the railing, just goes right up and over, tumbling into the water after her dog.

"Bridesmaid overboard!" someone calls, and several men run to the stern, one carrying a life preserver.

I rush to help, but when the man with the life preserver swings it behind him before heaving it into the water, I have to dodge out of the way. I stumble back and straight into the box the steering wheel is mounted on, where my elbow connects hard with a button.

KA-BAAM! POP! POW! BANG! BOOM!

The entire ten-minute fireworks display planned for the end of the reception explodes at one time from the barge on the starboard side of us.

Activated by me.

I stand frozen in place again, my wide eyes locked with my mother's, as a group of tuxedo-wearing men haul a dripping mermaid/bridesmaid/whatevermaid and her soggy dog out of the water. At least the pouch with the rings is still attached to his collar.

But that thing I said about being really good at my job? Maybe not so much today.

Mom likes to borrow a theater saying when she talks about her "event philosophy": The show must go on. I'm pretty sure she's never had to apply it quite like this before. I clean up belowdecks and then hang back as much as I can, trying to help without getting in the way. Mom barely even acknowledges me as she rushes around doing wedding-planner stuff, but when she does catch my eye, I see the way her lips tug down into a frown. Each time it happens, my stomach has that hollow feeling you get when you just know you are so completely in for it once everyone else leaves.

The ceremony resumes where it left off and is pretty uneventful except for Max/Shep shaking himself dry at the top of the aisle during the you-may-now-kiss-the-bride part. Luckily for us, once people get over the shock—and after Mom changes the bridesmaid into a backup mermaid dress (only two sizes too small)—things start looking up (not for me, but at least for the guests). The bridesmaid calls her mom to come to the marina, and we send the horrible-smelling wet dog back to the mainland on the dinghy. He's joined by the still-puking photographer.

By the last toast of the night, the video of the entire incident, which one of the groomsmen wasted no time posting to YouTube, has 244,365 hits. By the last dance at sunset, the bride and groom have agreed to detour to Wilmington on their way to the honeymoon in order to discuss their "hilarious wedding disaster" on the local morning show.

All's well that ends well? Not where Mom's concerned, I'm guessing. The chug of the departing dinghy signals the official end of the reception. The only people left on the boat now, besides me and Mom, are the caterers cleaning up and Izzy, who's gone back to her book down below.

Mom crosses the deck and points me into a chair near the giant Prince Eric ice sculpture.

"I'm so sorry, Mom," I say before she can get a word out.

She sighs and reaches for my hand. "I know you are, baby, and I understand how it happened."

Her smile is the kind that doesn't go all the way into her eyes, which are a little sad-looking. I stare back into them as she says, "On the other hand, I have the reputation of my business to think about, and I have to put that first."

Ahead of me?

I drop my eyes to my lap. Mom sighs again. "Sweetness, maybe twelve is just too young to be handling everything I've asked of you. Maybe we need to rethink things a little bit."

Wait a minute. Am I getting fired? By my own *mother*? This cannot be happening.

"You've been a huge help to me, Sadie. You know that. But this mistake is going to cost the company thousands of dollars after I refund the bride's dad for the fireworks show he paid for. Plus we lose any referrals that bride could have given us. I just hope she doesn't mention my company by name on television Monday morning."

She tucks me under her arm and gives me a squeeze. I keep my body stiff when she says, "I'm not mad, Sades. It's my fault for giving you so much responsibility. Summer's just starting. You should spend it doing kid stuff. Fun stuff. Not dealing with all this stress."

Does she not remember the whole reason I started working with her is because I DO find it fun? Well, at first it was just because it was a chance to be with Mom, but it turns out I'm really good at it . . . most days. I'm the one who came up with the idea for the ice sculpture to match the statue in the movie. And it was me who tracked down the sheet music for "Kiss the Girl" for the wedding band. I love coming up with fun details to make the weddings memorable and I *thought* Mom loved it too. She's always going on about what a huge help I am to her.

I didn't notice anyone *else* thinking to bring a blender for that groom who'd had emergency dental surgery the morning of the wedding, so he could still have some wedding cake. Or finding weights to clip onto the bridesmaids' dresses' hems when we had an outdoor wedding on the beach during a super-windy day. And, I mean, it's not like I haven't made some little mistakes at a wedding before. There was the time I accidentally left with the keys to the reception site and the florist couldn't get in early to do the centerpieces. But I rode my bike over as fast as I could the second she called. Maybe tonight's was a little more . . . severe, but in the past Mom's always understood that events might have wrinkles.

It stinks to be unappreciated, but what's even worse

is being entirely invisible. Which is exactly what I'll be if she fires me. I'll fade back into the wallpaper like before.

I nod hard against Mom's chest so she won't catch on that I'm trying not to let the tears spill over. We're interrupted by the caterer, who needs her to sign some form, which leaves me free to slide my phone from my pocket and scroll through all my emoticons until I find the tiny pair of bat wings. I type it into a group text to my three best friends.

There. Bat signal sent.

It cheers me up a tiny bit to picture all of them heading for their bikes (or golf cart, for Lauren, depending on where she is at the marina) and pointing them to our Bat Cave. Well, our Bat Boat, if we're being technical.

I stand, cross the deck, and yell down to Izzy that I'm catching the next dinghy shuttle to shore. As I board the tiny boat, the last thing I hear is someone from the catering staff humming "Part of Your World" as she cleans up. Too bad my chance to be part of Mom's world exploded alongside those fireworks.

2

Lauren

irk verb \ˈərk\
to annoy, bother, or make irritated
Use in a sentence:
My brother irks me when I'm trying to study and
he's playing Death War 3000 at top volume.

I'm memorizing the definition of "cerebral" ("of or
relating to the brain or intellect") when my phone sings
out the theme to Batman. So I do what any best friend
would—even one who has to memorize the definitions
of fifty new SAT vocab words for prep class this week. I
put down the flash cards and check my texts.

No words, just the bat signal. Which means only
one thing: BFF meeting, ASAP.

"Can you watch the office for a while?" I ask Zach
as I grab my flash cards, my phone, and this amazing

pink-and-maroon scallop shell I found on the beach earlier. I stuff them all into my backpack.

"I'm busy," my video-game-playing older brother says. Between him and Josh, my oldest brother who's off at college taking summer classes to make up for everything he failed last semester, my brothers could hold the world record for number of hours spent slacking. The screen on the marina's office TV blasts a bright red TERMINATED at Zach.

I zap the thing off. "Not anymore. Give me an hour, tops."

Zach pushes his rolling chair back to the desk. The lamplight shines off his newly shaved head. He thinks he looks like LeBron James. But what he really looks like is a younger, skinnier, browner version of Dad—minus the boat-patterned shirts.

"We'll be closed in an hour. Has anyone ever told you how annoying you are?" Zach says.

"You. Every day." I make for the door and step out into the sticky June night.

I bypass the golf cart parked out front and race down the dock toward the *Purple People Eater*. It's not an actual purple people eater, obviously. It's the name of the sad old lavender-colored yacht Dad bought a few years ago for barely anything. He keeps talking about fixing it up and selling it, but until he gets around to that, it makes a pretty nice spot for four twelve-year-old girls to hang out on.

Fishing boats and yachts are coming in for the night at Sandpiper Beach Marina. I wave at the people onboard as I run past. When your dad owns the only marina in town, you get to know everyone who has a boat. At the very end of the dock, the peeling paint and rusty spots of the *Purple People Eater* disappear in the dim lights. I hop aboard just as the sweeping glow from the lighthouse rolls past and unlock the cabin door. Why Dad actually keeps it locked, I have no idea. It's not like anyone would want to steal this thing.

By the time Sadie pokes her head in, I've got the little bucket of flashlights all lit and sitting in the middle of the floor, plus snacks and bottles of water set out. It's about a hundred degrees inside, so I've opened all the windows to try to catch a breeze.

"You beat Vi here," I say.

"The *Little Mermaid* wedding was tonight, remember? Those tiny dinghy shuttles are fast." Sadie plops onto the floor and digs into a bag of pretzels.

The glow from the flashlights hits her face. I've been

friends with Sadie since preschool, and I can tell when something's not right. She just looks . . . off. I hand her a bottle of water.

"Sades, what's wrong?"

"That's why I called the meeting." She takes a gulp of water and makes a face. "Why is this warm?"

"No electricity on the *Purple People Eater*, remember? So what happened?"

"Can we wait for everyone else to get here?" She drags a hand across her eyes, and I reach over and give her a hug. She sort of slumps when I let go. Something is definitely wrong.

Vi sprints down the steps. She's wearing her summer uniform—running shorts, a tank top, and flip-flops. And her long blond hair is dripping wet in its ponytail.

"Were you swimming? It's almost dark outside," I say. Seriously, Vi's in the ocean so much that one day she's going to turn into a mermaid. Now, *that* would've been perfect for the wedding Sadie was at—a real, live mermaid swim-by.

"Bat signal came when I was in the shower. I had to get the beach volleyball sweat off. But look what I brought!" She holds out a small plastic bag.

I peek inside. "Pita chips!" I grab the bag and have a

chip in my mouth before Vi can say anything else. She makes some seriously amazing food, but the homemade pita chips are my all-time, absolute, forever favorite. They never taste the same twice because she's always messing with the recipe.

"I tried sea salt this time," she says.

"Like from the ocean?" Sadie asks.

I stop chewing for a second. The chips are really, really good, but no way am I eating gross ocean salt.

Vi laughs. "Yeah, but they sell it in the store. It's not like I took a bucket down to the beach or anything." I must be making a weird face, because Vi looks at me and says, "It's totally safe, I promise. And kind of good for you too."

I decide to trust her and start chewing again.

Vi joins Sadie on the floor and opens a bottle of water. "Yuck, this isn't cold!"

"No electricity," I say again. Maybe I should rethink this whole providing-snacks-and-beverages-at-the-Bat-Cave thing and put Vi in charge of it instead.

"Knock, knock! Miss me?" Becca floats down the narrow steps.

"Sorry I sent the signal in the middle of your Visitor's Center reception thingy," Sadie says.

Becca's parents are in charge of the Sandpiper Beach Visitor's Center. Technically, they run an association of all the businesses in our town, but they also have a little glassed-in kiosk where tourists can get brochures and directions to the closest bathroom and facts about local history (which aren't always correct—I mean, the lighthouse was built in 1857, not 1859 like I heard her dad tell someone last week). That's where they're always hanging out, which irritates Becca to no end.

I see her point, though. Sandpiper Beach has a population of 4,042 (in the winter, at least—that number quintuples when the summer crowds show up—and that's being nice and including the part of the town that's actually on the mainland, across the bridge), so pretty much everyone knows everyone else's business already. But when your parents are in a glass box in the center of town 24/7, they *really* know everything that's going on.

Becca waves her hand. "Ugh, it was sooooo seriously boring. Deadly. Except at the very end when this completely adorable guy showed up with Mrs. O'Malley. I think he was her grandson or something. I was *thisclose* to working my way over to him when my phone buzzed. Lo, are you planning to share those or not?"

I take just one more pita chip and reluctantly pass the bag to Becca.

"Wait, there's a guy who exists in this town and you don't know every single detail about him? How is that even possible?" Vi draws up her knees and rests her chin on them, grinning at Becca.

Becca's quest for a boyfriend began the day she turned twelve and decided she was officially old enough for one. So far she hasn't had the best luck, which probably has a lot to do with the whole population 4,042 thing and the fact that everyone in our grade has known each other since we wore swim diapers while building our sand castles.

"Now I have to go all Nancy Drew and track him down. Who's with me on this?" Becca seems ready to whip out a notepad and a magnifying glass, detective-style.

"Could we talk about guys later, maybe?" Sadie says.

Becca squints in the dim flashlight glow. "Have you been crying?"

"Sadie, what happened?" Vi scoots closer and wraps a long, tanned arm around Sadie.

"Mom fired me."

"She *what*?!" Becca says. She's got this look on her

face like Cute New Guy just told her he has a girlfriend.

"How? Why? Wait, does this have something to do with all those fireworks that went off tonight?" I grab Sadie's hand. Working with her mom's wedding-planning business means—meant—*everything* to Sadie. It's so different from me working in the marina office. I'm only here because Dad pays me, not because I'm super into boats.

"Yeah, that was kind of my fault. All the fireworks went off at the same time, a bridesmaid and her dog went overboard, a gull pooped in my hair, the happy couple is going on a morning show to do a tell-all, and Mom doesn't want me working with her anymore." Sadie's not really looking at any of us.

"A seagull pooped in your hair?" Becca couldn't look more horrified. Sadie nods and Becca shudders. "I'd die. Die! So dead."

Vi's hiding her face, and I just know she's trying really hard not to laugh. I'm sure it's more at the thought of a bird pooping in Becca's hair than at what actually happened to Sadie.

"But you're so good at planning and organizing and coming up with really creative stuff. The anchor invitations you designed for the marina's Christmas party were Mom and Dad's favorite thing ever. And all the costumes you pulled together for the *Little Women* production at school last year? Everyone was talking about them," I say. "You need to show your mom that she can't live without your help."

"Exactly," Vi adds. She's tossing the bottle of warm water up in the air and catching it, like it's a weirdly shaped baseball. "Hey, you should totally plan a wedding on your own and remind her how great you are at party planning!"

"Yeah, something totes better than a *Little Mermaid* wedding, too. Something so, so, so ah-mazing that the bride and groom would pay you, like, a gazillion billion dollars because you're giving them the wedding they only wished they'd dreamed about," Becca says.

"Like the one you're already planning for yourself and Visitor's Center Guy?" Sadie's actually smiling now.

Becca shrugs. "No. Maybe."

"But who would hire a twelve-year-old to plan a wedding?" I ask. "Even though you'd be awesome at it, Sades."

Becca leans forward. "Maybe not a wedding. But what about some other kind of party, like a birthday?"

Sadie's face lights up. "I could do that." Her face falls

again. "But none of us have birthdays coming up."

"But I know exactly who *could* use a little birthday-party-planning help." Becca pulls a business card from her pocket and passes it across the flashlights to Sadie. "While I was watching the new guy scarf cheese and crackers at the social tonight, Mrs. Campbell was going on and on to my parents about booking the Poinsettia Plantation House for her daughter's birthday party, except all they had available was next Saturday afternoon, and how could she organize a party in that short amount of time, and blabbity blah blah. She seemed really freaked out about it. Of *course* Mom volunteered me to help with the kids during the party." Becca rolls her eyes.

Sadie gazes at the business card. "I could plan that, if Mrs. Campbell would let me. But there's no way I can do it by myself."

"We'll help." Vi leans back to catch her water-bottle baseball. "Becca, can you call her now?"

"Really? You're all into this?" Sadie looks around the circle at us.

"Of course," Vi says.

"Definitely." I'm trying not to think of everything else I have to get done this week—SAT study class, working at the marina, volunteering at the homeless shelter in Wilmington on Thursday, and playing Bunco with my grandmother and her friends at Sandpiper Active Senior Living on Friday.

But Sadie is my best friend. And if she needs help planning a party, I don't care how many things I have to move around in my schedule to make that happen.

The pink rhinestones on Becca's phone case sparkle in the flashlight beams as she punches in Mrs. Campbell's number. I reach over the flashlights and quietly pull the bag of pita chips back across the floor. That sea-salt stuff isn't so bad.

"Hi? Mrs. Campbell? This is Becca Elldridge. . . . What? Oh. Yes, Mom and Dad *are* godsends to this town. . . ." Becca's fighting another eye roll, I can totally see it. "Saturday at two . . . well, that's exactly what I'm calling about. . . ."

Vi's poking Becca in the knee with the end of her water bottle and mouthing *speakerphone*. Becca shakes her head.

"You see, I have this amazing friend, Sadie Pleffer . . . you know her? Yeah, she's pretty great, isn't she?" Becca smiles at Sadie, whose face is turning red. "So it turns out she's really awesome at party planning. Yup, just like her mom! I'm sorry, what?"

Becca's nodding and saying "mmm-hmm" a lot. I'm dying to say "What?" already, but that's super annoying when you're trying to talk to someone on the phone. Not that Vi cares about that. She's poking Becca's knee again and whispering, "What? What's she saying?"

Becca swats at Vi's hand. "I think we can help you with that. Well, Sadie mostly . . . sure, you can talk to her." She passes Sadie the phone.

Sadie's face changes into an exact copy of her mom's when she's in wedding mode. "Hi, Mrs. Campbell?" After a pause, Sadie launches into a description of all the things she used to do for her mother's business. "And we'll take care of the cake, the decorations, the entertainment, everything! All you have to do is show up with Molly. I just need to know how much we can, um, spend. Oh, wow, really?" She points at my backpack and mimes writing something.

I scrounge in my bag and pass her my lucky test-taking pen and a notebook. Sadie scribbles as she listens, and then she hangs up with Mrs. Campbell after telling her thank you about a million times.

"So? What did she say?" Vi's put the water bottle down and is twisting the damp ends of her ponytail around her finger.

"She said . . . yes!" Sadie couldn't smile any bigger if she tried.

Becca pounces on Sadie and bear-hugs her. "You're going to be a real, official party planner!"

"*We* are," Sadie says.

"Of course!" I say. "Um, details, please?"

"Oh, right! So the party is at Poinsettia Plantation over on the mainland on Saturday at two. It's for Mrs. Campbell's daughter Molly, who will be nine. She told me to 'have at it.' Her budget is . . . well . . ."

Becca waves a hand. "They're mega-rich, we know."

"Right. And—get this—she's going to pay us!" Sadie's face is flushed red in the glow of the flashlights.

"Like, actual money?" Vi asks.

"No, Monopoly money. Of course it's actual money, silly!" Becca teases. "So, what kind of theme, Sades?"

Sadie taps her hand on her knee. "Have y'all seen the porch at that house? It's huge, and they have all those little tables and chairs. It would be perfect for a fancy tea party."

"Ooh, with all different kinds of tea and a big cake!" Wait, did that just come out of my mouth? Okay, maybe I'm a little more excited about this party-planning thing than I thought.

"I love that place. It's like straight out of *Gone with the Wind*," Becca says. "The porch reminds me of the very beginning, you know, where Scarlett flirted with those red-haired boys?" She waves a hand at her face, like she's Scarlett O'Hara fanning herself.

"Um, I've never seen *Gone with the Wind*," Vi says.

"You *what*!? Okay, just trust me on this. That place is so *Gone with the Wind*," Becca says.

"Yeah, I think it actually looks more like a haunted house," I say.

"Haunted by the ghosts of Southern belles past, you mean," Becca says.

"Murdered Southern belles. I swear those windows look like dark, empty eyes." I actually kind of hate going by there at night, but I keep that to myself. I know ghosts can't really exist. It's not logical. But still . . . the ground lights they use make the house look all tall and twisted. And there are all these vines and Spanish moss. It's super creepy. As long as we have the party on the porch during the day, I think I'll be okay. Logical or not, I refuse to go inside. Period.

"Lauren, I can't believe you're not writing all this down." Sadie picks the notebook and pen back up.

"If I wasn't completely freaked out by the idea of Civil War ghosts crashing a birthday party, then maybe I'd be taking notes." I shiver, even though it's still hot and stuffy inside the *Purple People Eater*, despite the open windows.

Sadie writes something and then lays the notebook down on the yacht floor next to the flashlights.

Vi leans forward to read, and her ponytail swings over her shoulder. "Tea, Southern belles, and murdered ghosts. Ooo-*kay*."

"The murdered ghosts thing wasn't an actual idea. More like a reason I'm glad we're doing this during the day." I reach for my pen to cross out the ghosts, but Sadie pulls it away.

"Wait," she says. "This could work."

We all just look at her.

"No, really!" Sadie's got her planning face on—the one that's smiles and concentration at the same time. "See, tea and pretty dresses go great together, but that's going to entertain nine-year-olds for what, like five minutes? But . . . if we turn it into a murder-mystery party . . ."

"Ohhh!" Vi says. "Like those games you can buy,

where someone's a 'murderer' and everyone has to put the clues together and figure out who it is?"

"Exactly! And if we can act out the murder scene, they'll love it even more." Sadie's already scribbling more notes.

"Wait, what do you mean by 'we'?" I say. "There's no way I'm acting anything out. No, nada, uh-uh."

Becca leaps up. "I call the part of the murdered person!" Becca mimes pulling a knife out of her stomach, rolls her eyes back, and collapses into a heap next to the warm water bottles. Then she sits straight up. "All I need is a cute someone who could catch me as I die and weep over my dead body."

"Becca, you're definitely the most dramatic one here, that's for sure. Don't worry. We'll have a part for you," Sadie says. Her brain is obviously in mega-organizer mode.

I cross my arms. "I am *not* acting anything. Y'all act. I'll be the narrator or whatever."

"We'll figure that out later," Sadie says. "Is everyone okay with a Southern murder-mystery tea party?"

We all nod, and Becca offers to call Mrs. Campbell to run it by her. Then Sadie makes a list of things to do and we split it up.

Becca's phone buzzes just as Sadie checks off the last to-do assignment. "It's Daddy," Becca says. "I guess he's all done tending to his sheep."

Sadie looks at her sideways.

"All the business owners in the chamber of commerce. Dad says they're like his flock. Please, if he had real sheep, can you imagine the fabulous sweater collection I would have? Anyway, I gotta bolt. If I'm not home by nine thirty, he'll totally murder me and not even care that the crime would keep tourists away. Smooches!"

Becca takes off, with Vi right behind her. I gather up the trash—including Vi's empty pita-chip bag—and lock up the *Purple People Eater* before Sadie and I walk back to the office.

"So we're really doing this," she says.

"Yup. This party is going to be amazing. Just wait till your mom sees you in action. She'll wish she never fired you. Hold up, I want to give you something." In the yellow-colored light streaming down from the lamppost next to us, I dig through my backpack until I find what I'm looking for.

I hold the beautiful pink-and-maroon shell out to Sadie. "Here, I found this today. Scallop shells are symbolic of pilgrimages. And maybe you're on a new journey. I mean, I know that's not the same thing as a pilgrimage, since a pilgrimage is religious and all, but . . ."

Sadie's trying really hard not to laugh, I can tell.

"Anyway, it's really pretty, isn't it?"

Sadie takes the shell and admires it in the light. "Thanks, Lo." And her grin is brighter than the moon overhead. It might even be brighter than all those fireworks she set off earlier.

And that makes me happier than any A on a test ever could.

3

Becca

Daily Love Horoscope for Scorpio:
Venus is rising. It's the perfect day to go flirt
with a cute stranger.

As soon as I'm old enough, I'm totes packing up and
moving somewhere like Savannah, because this Southern belle look is soooo completely me. I twist my neck
so I can watch myself sway from behind in the full-length
mirror on the back of my bedroom door. Omigosh, *why*
did petticoats ever go out of style? I mean, okay, fine,
they're not the most comfortable things to wear in the
middle of, like, the single most humid June on record,
but they swish when I walk.

SWISH. When I walk.

I *realllly* need to put this dress back in my closet so it doesn't get ruined before next week's party because Sadie would KILL me after she was up first thing this morning talking the janitor into opening the school so we could borrow the costumes from *Little Women*. With a few tweaks they're perfect Southern belle dresses. Okay, off it goes. But maybe just one or two more swishes first. *Swish. Swish. Swish.* Last one, I swear. *Swish.*

Except . . . this dress would give me the perfect excuse to find the cute boy from the Visitor's Center social the other night and position myself right in front of him before murmuring, "I do declare, I'm feeling right faint in this heat." And then I can swoon directly into his arms and he'll realize he's been looking for a girlfriend like me his whole life and he'll have to revive me to tell me just that.

So romantic.

And just like that, I think of a possible song. I always get this buzz when I hit on an idea I'm excited about, and it's like it *hums* through me as I grab my spiral notebook from under my pillow and flip past the giant PRIVATE on the cover. I turn sheets until I find a blank one and scribble "plantation," "petticoat dress," and "love like ours never goes out of fashion" to jog my memory when I have time to work on it later, maybe with my guitar. I snap the notebook closed, but then find the page again quickly when a lyric comes to me out of the blue. I write,

> When I doubt,
> You surprise me.
> When I faint,
> You revive me.

I promise, promise, promise myself I'll go back to that page later. But I have my fingers crossed just in case that whole Pinocchio thing is true. My nose is totes my best feature and I don't need it growing all long on me. Eww.

Anyway, it's not like I don't *want* to go back to it. I want to go back to *all* my pages of scribbles and turn them into something amazing. Something you could hear on the radio and just have to hum along to.

I jam my notebook under the pillow as hard as I can.

Because the problem is that all those song lyrics are about L-O-V-E. And I . . . don't know anything about that. My English teacher said the very best writers always write what they know and write from the heart.

Um, hello? My heart is twelve. I barely know my *times tables* inside and out.

But having a boyfriend, a boyfriend who adores me and inspires me and makes me feel all the feels, would solve that. *That's* why I need one. My friends think I just want a boyfriend to be cool (and also plus because I *might* have a reputation for being a teeny-tiny bit boy-crazy ever since first grade, when Christopher Paulson picked me to march next to him in the kazoo band in the Fourth of July parade), but really I have REASONS. I just haven't been able to bring myself to tell them those reasons.

Which is admittedly weird. One, because I truly, positively, absolutely know Sades, Vi, and Lo would have my back and most likely even think songwriting is really cool and completely perfect for me. Two, because I'm like the least shy person I know when it comes to pretty much everything else. Mama says I'm "deliciously flamboyant"; Daddy says I'm "responsible for all the antacids I take." (Which he always says with a smile, so I know he doesn't actually mean that. Probably.)

But my songs are different. They're just so *personal* on this, like, really deep level that makes me weirdly shy about them. It would be completely squicky-feeling to let anyone read my lyrics. Omigosh, I would die!

Okay, so *that* just got real. Time to shake it off. I slide from my bed and kind of can't help pausing in front of the mirror again to admire the dress. So faint-worthy. I wonder what smelling salts smell like. The salt I use on my corn on the cob doesn't really have an odor, but all the girls wearing swishy dresses in old movies are always getting revived from their fainting spells by smelling salts. Weird. Probably Cute Boy doesn't walk around with salt in his pocket. Then again, I'll never know if I don't give him the chance.

Sending a silent promise to Sadie that I'll be extra careful in the dress, I bounce down the steps.

"Rebecca Elise Elldridge. *What* are you wearing?"

I skid to a stop with one hand on the front door. Drat. I was two seconds from freedom.

"Daddy, it's a dress, of course."

"I can see that it's a dress, Rebecca, but what I would like to know is *why* you are planning to wear a dress like that out and about?"

"I just . . ." I wonder if Mama ever swooned in Daddy's arms. Ew. Gross. I really, really will not discuss swooning with my *father*.

"I don't expect this will be the last time we have this

conversation," Daddy says, dropping his voice before mumbling, "Lord knows it isn't the first." Then his voice gets all normal again. "Your mother and I are the first people most visitors encounter when they get here. We're the face of this town. The business owners on the chamber of commerce count on us to make them look good. As our daughter, the same goes for you, young lady. Now march."

He extends his arm and points my way back up the steps.

Le sigh.

I spin in place and lift my chin as I pass him, making sure to put some extra stomp in my step as I navigate the stairs and head back to my room. I toss the swishy dress on my gingham bedspread and switch to a pair of yellow twill shorts and a magenta cami.

"Bye, Daddy." I wave as I glide downstairs. He nods his approval and heads back to his home office while I close the door behind me, race down the stairs, and cross under the house to the storage room. I roll my bike out and pedal toward the beach at top speed, almost like I'm on a mission.

Okay, I'm totally on a mission.

Technically, it's to get supplies so the girls and I can

fold tea-party fans and cut out tea-party doilies at the *Purple People Eater* tonight, but that's not my main goal for today. Nope. *Today* is the day I scope out Hottie McHottington, the new boy in town. Fresh blood is hard to come by when you live in a beach town that is less like a dot on a map and more like the fleck of pepper that fell onto it. Granted, we get the summer tourist crowds, but they're usually weekly renters, and who wants a boyfriend who'll be packing up his boogie board by noontime Saturday? No thanks. I need a *real* relationship that will help my songs feel more . . . authentic. It totally works for Taylor Swift.

I pedal harder to work out my frustration. Operation Get a Boyfriend, which was *supposed* to be Mission Complete by now, is in danger of becoming Mission Impossible if I don't step it up, and fast.

It's possible Cute Boy is a weekly too, but he seemed pretty chummy with Mrs. O'Malley, and even though the weeklies are always venturing into the Visitor's Center for restaurant reservations or to rent a fishing boat, I'm pretty positive I've never seen one at a business chamber social.

So this leaves me with a mystery to solve. The Mystery of the Mystery Guy. I'm like Nancy Drew.

Or Encyclopedia Brown. Or maybe even Dora the Explorer without a backpack singing to me. I'm like Daphne from Scooby— Oh, wait. Um, I think that's him walking on the road to the beach up ahead. Okay, so that wasn't the world's best detective work, but hey, it's all about the results, not the procedure, right?

I slow my bike so I can observe from behind. Hmm. Definitely looks like the same messy-in-a-boy-band-way hair, not messy in an I-don't-own-a-comb-way hair. It's the exact coppery brown color with little streaks of blond I drooled over at the Visitor's Center. I could *definitely* write a lyric or two about that hair.

And his eyes! He's facing away from me, so I can't tell if they're the piercing blue I remember. It feels like mere days ago that we were locking gazes across the racks of brochures for hot-air balloon rides and water parks. Okay, so it *was* mere days ago. Or, well, yesterday.

Anyway, I don't need to see his baby blues, because the fact that he's wearing the same orange T-shirt he had on last night is probably evidence enough. How many other middle-school-aged guys in town could possibly have a T-shirt with MRS. POPPOT'S SCHOOL OF DRAMA. STOP "ACTING" LIKE IT'S ALL ABOUT YOU! stamped across the back? I'm pretty sure Dora could crack this case even without Backpack's help.

I pedal slowly behind him as I collect more data. Bare feet, but picking his way along the sandy side of the road, so probably not used to walking without shoes. Definitely *not* a local. Towel, rolled up and slung around his neck. Striped board shorts.

I use my thumb to pull back the tab on the little bell attached to my handlebars as soon as we've both crossed Coastline Drive and passed the pavilion. When it *brrring-brrring*s, Mystery Boy jumps a little and scoots toward the edge of the boardwalk leading to the beach, but he doesn't turn around. How are we supposed to have our Meet Cute like in the movies if he won't even turn around? Rude.

Well, a girl has to make a memorable first impression, right? So I do the only thing I can think of.

I crash into him.

I mean, I slow down as much as possible so I don't actually hurt him or anything, but I guess getting tapped from behind by a beach cruiser when you aren't expecting it is kind of enough to knock someone off his feet. I'm so surprised at his yelp that I'm thrown off balance too, and I go tumbling over the handlebars and land beside him in the marshy grass lining the boardwalk. Whoops.

His lips form a shocked O shape. But all I can focus on are those blue, blue eyes. Seriously, they are like something out of . . . out of . . . whatever's really, really, *really* blue. Just picture that.

"Sorry!" I say, when I tear my eyes away from all that epic blueness.

"'Sorry'? 'Sorry' is all you can say? You ran me over!"

Oh. My. Gosh. He. Has. An. Accent.

British, I think. Or Irish, maybe? Is there anything more swoon-worthy *ever*? I am so working this into the song about us. I wonder if he would read the phone book to me. Probably not the best time to ask him, because he looks a little, um, perturbed. Is that a word? I think it is. I'll have to ask Lauren.

I stand up, brushing sand from my knees. "Well, it was an accident. Geez. Anyway, hey! I'm Becca!" I stick my hand out but he ignores it.

"Do you always meet lads by running them over?" he asks.

I mean, no, but it's not the worst idea ever.

I give him my sweetest smile. "I didn't run you over.

I bumped into you . . . with my bike. Totally different. Anyway, like I said, it was an accident."

He still looks super annoyed as he grabs his towel from the ground and loops it back around his neck. He uses one end of the terry cloth to swipe sand from the top of his sunscreen bottle, which is how I really, *really* know he's not from around here. Any local could tell you that getting sand off an opened sunscreen bottle is a lost cause.

"So, um, I saw you at the Visitor's Center the other night. Are you Mrs. O'Malley's grandson or something?"

"Or something," he answers, now brushing sand from his elbow.

Geez. He's really annoyed. If it weren't for those blue (cobalt? Is that a thing?) eyes and that accent, I might give up on this one. Maybe I'll learn all about L-O-V-E from a book instead. I point to his T-shirt.

"Drama camp, huh? Are you an actor?"

He heaves a (very dramatic, one might say) sigh and his eyebrows smoosh down. "Trying to be. I'm supposed to be at camp right now working on my craft. But me mum and da had to run some research trip and they deposited me here with me great-aunt."

Accent. Accent! Wait, whoops. I was so busy listening

to the way he formed his words that I didn't actually hear them. Something about aunts and research.

"That's nice," I say with a ginormous smile.

He cocks his head and looks at me sort of funny, then gives a little shake and turns back to the beach. "Thanks again for running me over," he calls over his shoulder.

Whoa. He did not just turn his back on me, did he? I stand with my jaw dropped open for a second, watching him start up the boardwalk.

This is so not over.

Vi

HOMEMADE PITA CHIPS

Ingredients:

3 pieces of pita bread

4 tbsp olive oil

1 clove of garlic, smashed

salt and pepper, to taste

Preheat over to 375 degrees. Cut pitas into 8 wedges each and place on a baking sheet. Brush each wedge with olive oil and garlic. Season with salt and pepper. Bake for 12–15 minutes.

**If Lauren is around, double this recipe.*

**Don't eat these before talking to Linney, or she'll sniff the air and act like she's allergic to garlic. She's probably a vampire.*

*A*n army of plastic bride and groom cake toppers grin at me, like they know I have zero idea what I'm doing.

Okay, not *zero* idea. I mean, I know I'm ordering a cake, and I have a whole list of pictures and instructions from Sadie to go along with it. But this place is So Not Vi. It's all pastel and frou-frou, and it smells like a hundred Pixy Stix exploded inside. This whole party is So Not Vi, so it's not like that should be a surprise. And I have to put myself into one of those prissy, fluffy costume dresses. If I get stuck with the pink one that looks like wearable cotton candy, I will NOT be happy. I'd do anything to help Sadie, but that's really asking too much.

I shiver in the AC—it's turned up so high that I'm really thankful I have contacts now instead of glasses that would fog up the second I stepped back outside—and glance down the length of the glass display case. Mrs. Marks, the owner of Marks Makes Cakes, is still busy with the same woman.

"Violet?" A sniffy little voice says from behind me.

I know that voice. And it makes me want to roll my eyes and run away at the same time. Only two people call me Violet—my meemaw and Linney Marks.

"You're dripping all over the floor." Linney points at the pink linoleum, which is dotted with drops of water.

As she slips behind the display case, I twist my ponytail up. Totally wrong choice, because even more salty ocean water squeezes onto the floor. I really should cut my hair. A cute little bob or pixie style would be way more practical for swimming and volleyball. But I kind of secretly think that long hair is prettier.

Not that I'd admit that to anyone.

"Um, sorry. I was swimming and then I had to come here and . . ." Yeah. Not sure why I'm trying to explain myself.

Linney's just standing there in her dry yellow sundress and dry highlighted hair, eying my drippy ponytail and soaked-through T-shirt and running shorts like I've committed crimes against fashion. Maybe I should've gone home and changed instead of pulling my clothes over my swimsuit. That's something Becca would know to do. She's always trying to lend me dresses or curl my hair or attack me with some piece of makeup.

But at least Becca's nice about it. Linney—not so much. In fourth grade, I invited a bunch of girls in our class over for a sleepover. I'd never thought it was weird to live in Sandpiper Pines Mobile Home Park. I mean,

Dad and I had always lived there, and Mom too, before she left to "follow her dreams" in California. Whatever that means. But I barely remember her.

Anyway, the second Linney's mom dropped her off in front of our trailer, everything changed between us. She frowned at the rust spots outside that Dad kept meaning to sand off and repaint but never could because he worked so much. She perched on the kitchen chair inside like it might swallow her whole. And she refused to eat any of the spaghetti and homemade marinara sauce I'd cooked. (That was some good marinara too. I'd just figured out that if you add sugar to it, it totally changes the way the sauce tastes.)

Dad's always worked so much that he only ever had time to make mac and cheese from a box. That got really old after a while, so I taught myself how to cook. And it turned out that I really liked it. Cooking is like doing the best science experiment ever, or maybe a puzzle that has no right or wrong answer.

So, the next week at school after my party, Linney told everyone how I was "poor" and how sad it was that I had to live in an ugly trailer and maybe that's why I always wore running shorts and tanks. Which is so not true—that last part, anyway. The rest of it . . . I'm not so sure. I thought she might let up once Dad and I moved into Meemaw's nice beach house a couple of months ago, but she hasn't.

"So . . . why are you here? Isn't there some kind of game or meet or something you should be at?" Linney's not even looking at me. She's too busy rearranging the Bridal Battalion in the light-up display case.

I take a deep breath. I have to deal with Linney. For Sadie. When Linney made fun of my greenish-tinged pool hair last winter, Sadie accidentally-on-purpose knocked green paint onto Linney's brand-new jeans during art class. Best day ever.

"I need to order a cake from your mom," I finally say.

"I can take your order." Linney shuts the door to the case and opens a binder. "What flavor?" From somewhere behind the display case, she plucks a pink pen topped with—what else?—a cake.

"Linney?" Mrs. Marks has waved the other customer out the door. "I can take over."

"No, Mom," Linney barks. "I've got it."

Mrs. Marks scurries away toward the kitchen in the back.

Okaaay. That was kind of uncomfortable.

"It's sort of complicated." I push the pictures across to Linney. "It has to look like that plantation house in *Gone with the Wind*, with little trees and grass and stuff. And a tiny Scarlett and Rhett. Here's a picture of them."

"I *know* what Scarlett and Rhett look like." Linney writes something in the binder as I silently pull the pictures back and clutch them in front of me.

Linney taps the cake part of the pen on the page. She gives me the same pitying look she did the day everyone turned in their twenty dollars for the class field trip to Raleigh. Everyone but me, that is. (At least until Becca insisted she'd "just happened to find" a twenty when she was sweeping in the Visitor's Center.)

"This isn't going to be cheap, you know."

Okay. That's low. And how much do I hate that I can feel my face going red? Dad and I haven't lived in that trailer since April, but people like Linney will never forget it. I grit my teeth and don't say anything. For Sadie.

I look her straight in the eye. "This is for Molly Campbell's ninth birthday party. You know, the Campbells who built those new condos down by the mini-golf place? I can pay for it. It should say 'Happy Birthday, Molly,' and the cake needs to be chocolate. We'd like it delivered to the Poinsettia Plantation House on Saturday morning by eleven. Just call me if your mom has any questions. I have to get back to the beach for the volleyball game now."

And with that, I do my best Becca-inspired flounce right out the door—and turn the wrong way down the sidewalk. But Linney's either stunned into silence or not even looking, because she doesn't say anything as I flounce back by the Marks Makes Cakes window to grab my bike.

I unlock my bike from the rack and pedal fast through the square and toward the beach. Dealing with a monster like Linney totally earned me a detour by Beach Sports. I wish I knew how to stop letting her get under my skin. Dad says she'll forget all about it once we get to high school, but that's *ages* away. I roll past the souvenir T-shirt shop, and brake to a stop outside Beach Sports, where they've got all kinds of beachy sportiness displayed on the sidewalk to lure tourists to their cash registers.

Right there, side by side, next to a row of boogie boards, sit Vi's Most Wanted. Two kayaks in hunter green—Dad's favorite color. I'd put up with a hundred Linney Markses to get my hands on those. I've been saving my babysitting money since March. If I keep landing sitting gigs, Dad and I could be cutting through the water in those green kayaks by September.

Assuming I can get him away from work long enough, that is. Being in construction means you have to work a zillion hours a day, every day of the week. Unless it rains, then you don't work at all. And there's never enough money for things like kayaks or field trips or fancy ingredients from that ethnic grocery store that opened on the next island over. Dad always refuses to take the money Meemaw offers for stuff like that. Meemaw is my mom's mother, which makes things weird between her and Dad. He only agreed to move into her house because she'll be in Maine all summer and she didn't want to rent the place out. She told Dad he'd be doing her a favor by us moving in.

My phone buzzes in my pocket. It's lilac and So Not Vi, but it's a phone. Lauren's parents gave her a new one for her birthday, so she passed this one on to me. Embarrassing, but like I said, it's a phone. Which is better than no phone. And the lilac is maybe just a *little* bit cute.

Balancing over my bike, I click it on.

Hottie McH h8s me.

Becca.

I snort back a laugh. She has to mean that new guy she met at her parents' Visitors' Center thingy.

??? I type back.

Kinda sorta crashed into him.

Okay, now I laugh for real. Tourists give me funny looks as they wander by Beach Sports. Girl in wet clothes perched on a bike, laughing at her phone. I guess I do look a little crazy.

Why did u do that?

2 say hi.

Becca. Becca, Becca, Becca. Seriously, with all her know-how about clothes and makeup and stuff, she's completely clueless when it comes to actually talking to guys. Not that I really know a whole lot about boys either, but at least I know that running one over on your bike is probably not the best way to make friends.

"Vi?" Speaking of guys, Lance Travis, king of Sandpiper Beach Middle School sports, skids to a stop next to me. "Why aren't you at the beach? Major volleyball tournament, remember?"

I push off on my bike, down Coastline Drive, making sure to cut right in front of him when he starts pedaling again. He wobbles a bit and then rolls up next to me.

"Loser," he says, with his Lance-like half-smile that makes Becca sigh every time she walks by him.

"Butt breath," I say. "Did you find us a sixth person for our team?"

He rubs a hand through his short brown hair as he pedals. "Yeah, this Irish dude who showed up at the basketball courts in the park yesterday. Cruddy basketball player, but he swears he's good at volleyball."

"Great. Guess it's better than being down a player." My phone buzzes again. I glance at it, expecting Becca, but it's Sadie. "Hold up," I say to Lance.

He brakes and looks back at me. "You're stopping to text? Really? You're such a girl."

I punch him hard on the arm for that. "This is important. Just a sec."

Cake status? Sadie wants to know. She's probably sitting at her kitchen table, surrounded by charts and Post-it notes and whatever else super-organized people use to stay super organized.

Cake ordered, I type back.

Did they have mini S & R?

Whoops. In all my flouncing and dripping, I kind of forgot to make sure they had a little Scarlett and Rhett to stick on the cake. Linney said she knew what they looked like . . . so she would've told me if they didn't, right?

I hope so, anyway.

I know I should pedal back and find out for sure, but Lance is already giving me the evil eye for texting when I should be headed for the game. Okay, I'll just call later.

Yup. Don't worry! I type to Sadie.

"Vi! Volleyball, now! I'm leaving without you," Lance calls over his shoulder.

I shove the phone into the waistband of my shorts and take off after him. I'll call the cake shop after the game. No big deal.

YOU'RE INVITED

I do declare! Miss Molly Campbell, daughter of Jeremy and Christina Campbell, cordially invites you to her ninth birthday tea party—with a killer surprise twist!

The festivities shall take place at two o'clock on Saturday, June 27, at the Poinsettia Plantation House, 10370 Poinsettia Road, Sandpiper Beach (mainland).

Refreshments shall be provided. Formal dress encouraged.

Kindly RSVP to Sadie Pleffer at (910) 555-0110 or sadie@rsvpmail.com

5

Sadie

TODAY'S TO-DO LIST
- [ ] leave Mom reminder to come to Poinsettia Plantation House in her day planner
- [ ] finish taping paper fans
- [ ] pack fake blood

*B*ecs, are you kidding me with that dress right now?"

I love the girl to death, but who arrives to set up an event in petticoats? Even if it *is* at an old Southern plantation.

"But I swish when I walk." Becca's lower lip juts out in a perfectly lip-glossed pout, making it impossible to be mad. I puff my bangs out of my eyes.

"You look and *sound* fantastic, Swishy Girl. But I need you sweating, not *swishing* right now. There's a change of clothes in the emergency kit in the first upstairs bedroom. Top of the stairs, turn left," I tell her, pointing the way.

She gives me a grin and heads for the elaborate staircase. Halfway up she pauses and sweeps a hand across her forehead.

"Oh, Rhett, darling. Don't leave me."

"BECCA!" I place one hand on my hip and use my other to point more forcefully at the top of the stairs. I hope she's half as convincing later, when she has to be in character as a belle. I'm counting on her to help me make today extra perfect. I told Mrs. Campbell she'd be able to kick back and put her feet up because we'd handle everything and she'd seemed pretty into that. More importantly, I need Mom to witness the amazingness that is Party Planner Sadie so she'll realize she can't function without me, and that particular feat is going to take all our combined efforts. It has to be perfect by the time she arrives for her "surprise."

"Sadie, where do these go?" Vi is at my side, holding a stack of tablecloths.

At least I don't have to worry about Vi showing up in a hoop skirt. It's going to take a ton of coaxing to get her to change out of her flip-flops and board shorts into a Southern gentleman bachelor outfit as it is. She *claims* she's just happy she doesn't have to wear the cotton-candy dress, but we'll see when the time comes to get changed.

"The two rectangular ones are for the setups inside, then the round ones go on the tables on the porch," I answer, checking my clipboard.

"I'll do the outside ones," Lauren says. She probably wants to be alone out there so she can work math problems in her head as she sets up. I notice both of her feet are planted in the doorway.

"What are you, a vampire? Do you need an invitation to enter?" Vi grins as she teases Lauren.

"I'm not setting foot inside this . . . *unearthly* house if I can help it." Lauren gives an all-over body shudder.

Vi rolls her eyes and passes the tablecloths to Lauren, who pivots and strides across the deep porch. Lauren might find this house creepy, but I think it's pretty amazing. The ceilings in the entryway have to be like twenty feet tall. I bet I could stack all three of my friends on my shoulders and they still wouldn't touch the ceiling. Actually, though, it would probably need to be Vi on the bottom. She plays enough beach volleyball to have awesome shoulder muscles.

A staircase, wide enough for two girls wearing hoop

skirts to go up side by side, curves around as it reaches the second floor. The whole place is decorated super fancy, with enormous crystal chandeliers and green-and-gold magnolia-flower wallpaper covering every wall. There are more paintings of old-fashioned-looking people than I bet even Hogwarts has.

I guess if you stare at the portraits long enough, it does sort of look like the eyes are following you. Well, whatever. Most of the action will take place on the porch anyway. And that's completely amazing too. It wraps around the whole house and is big enough to ride bikes on.

Speaking of bikes . . .

I catch movement out the window and step closer to see a boy pedaling furiously up the tree-lined drive-way. I'm just reaching the porch steps when he skids to a halt in front of them.

"Am I late?" He's gasping for breath. Although . . . *nice accent.* I'm wondering if he rode all the way from the island. It's kind of a long bike ride. Lauren somehow guilted Zach into driving us and all our stuff out here, and Becca had her dad drop her off.

"Late for what?" I ask, but just then Vi appears behind me.

"Hey, Ryan, you made it! Sadie, this is Ryan."

Ooooo-*kay*. Am I missing something? I have every second of today mapped out in my event binder and I don't remember anything about any Ryan.

"Ryan just joined my beach volleyball team. I hired him to play the bachelor." Vi looks oh-so-proud of herself. "He's an actor, and I thought this would be the perfect gig for him."

Ryan bows at the waist, grinning. "I'm keen to put my skills to use. It's not quite drama camp, but it *is* an actual paid job, and a struggling actor never turns down a role."

Paid? I mouth to Vi, careful to angle myself so Ryan can't see my lips moving.

Just ten bucks, she mouths back, with a shrug. To Ryan she says, "We're really excited to have you here. I was supposed to play the bachelor, but I think it will be *much* more believable if he's actually, well, a *he*. You know, I sure hope you're better at acting than you are at volleyball." She crosses her arms and narrows her eyes at him. "If you lied about that, I'll make your life miserable."

Ryan smiles again and swings a leg over his bike so he's now standing next to it. "I promise I'm better at acting than I am at any sport."

I give Vi an uneasy look. "You know, Becca's been rehearsing that role with you like crazy. I hope she isn't too—"

"Well now, I do declare. Is that a real live gentleman I see?" Becca's green eyes are twinkling like a Christmas tree as she crosses the porch, still wearing, I might add, her swishy dress.

"—disappointed," I mumble. What was I thinking? Becca would never mind any change of plans, as long as a boy is involved.

"I daren't believe I caught your name the other day, fine sir," Becca says to Ryan, still using her over-the-top Southern drawl. Of course, on her it sounds adorable.

Too bad Ryan doesn't seem to think so. His grin fades a little as he mumbles, "Ryan."

Poor Becca. Looks like this guy isn't falling for her charms.

Although, what am I doing? I don't have time to worry about Becca's love life, or lack of one, because I have a party to prepare for. And it has to be the best, the most over-the-top, without-a-hitch Murder-Mystery/Southern-Tea-Party Birthday that's ever been thrown. Especially because Mom will be here to witness it.

I clap my hands. "We have thirty minutes before the guests arrive. Everyone back to work!"

Becca drops one hand onto the handlebar of Ryan's bike. "Let me show you where you can store this, Ryan." She swishes off with Ryan trailing her.

Vi giggles. "I'd hate to be that poor guy right now. Too bad he's not playing the corpse."

I glance at her and lift my eyebrows.

She smiles. "I have a feeling by the time we get to the murder part, he'll be begging for someone to shoot him."

"*Psst*, Sadie! You can't tell, can you?" Vi motions at her long skirt, which she's pulled up just slightly to reveal blue plastic flip-flops.

Oh, Vi. And she's still wearing the ponytail too, which I really doubt was a popular hairstyle in eighteen-hundred-whatever. Thing is, though, when she drops the skirt again, you really *can't* tell what's on her feet, and besides, how can I be annoyed when my friends are crazy awesome to be here helping me? Obviously, Vi would be way happier at the beach and Lauren probably has flash cards to fill out, and Becca . . . well, actually I'm sure Becca's perfectly content right here. But still.

I should be grateful to have friends who will sacrifice their day just so I can fix everything with my mom and get things back to normal.

I smile at Vi and give her a "whatever" shrug, then go back to filling a glass with pink lemonade for one of the guests on the porch. Tires crunch up the gravel drive and I jerk my head up to see if it's Mom's Volvo. It's not.

"Hey!" squeaks the girl I'm pouring a drink for, and I snap my attention back just before I overfill her cup.

"Sorry," I whisper.

Get your head in the game, Sadie. She'll be here. Besides, Mom showing up to see me dumping sugary beverages all over my guests won't exactly inspire her confidence in my ability to handle any party task she could throw at me. Which is what I have to prove today.

Lauren leans over my shoulder. "That's the last of the guests, by my head count. Any time you're ready."

As much as I want to wait for Mom to get here to begin, that wouldn't be fair to the birthday girl. I set the pitcher down gently and clap my hands together.

"Girls, if I could have everyone's attention."

Unfortunately, the group of nine-year-olds are so busy squealing over how fancy they all look in their dresses that no one pays me the slightest bit of attention. I try clapping again, but not one person looks my way.

The loudest whistle I've ever heard pierces the air. I swing my head towards Vi in time to see her remove two fingers from her mouth.

"Hi, y'all. This girl over here needs your attention for a few seconds before we can get back to the fun."

She points to me, and I barely manage to stop gaping at her and face the guests before they all turn their heads toward me.

"Um, hi. Hi, everyone. So, uh, we have a really fun afternoon planned for you, but, um, first we're going to start with some refreshments on the porch. So if the rest of you will please have a seat, we'll begin our tea service."

I don't know why I'm so nervous. I guess because when I help Mom my job is to mainly blend into the background as much as possible, but now I have to run the whole show. Talk about pressure. And just WHERE is my mother?

Forty-five minutes later, there's still no sign of her. But at least everything else is going smoothly. The tiny crustless finger sandwiches were a giant success (especially since I skipped traditional cucumber and made them peanut butter and jelly instead), and so was the sweet tea. The girls are fanning themselves with the folded paper fans Becca, Lauren, Vi, and I made the other night, and Molly and her mom both seem to be into the whole tea-on-the-porch thing.

I hate to admit it, but the biggest hit so far has been Ryan. He's completely owning his role as the gentleman of the house, welcoming each guest by name (the place cards I did totally come in handy) and pretty much charming the socks off of them. Looks like Becca is now gonna have to fight her way through a swarm of nine-year-olds if she wants a shot at him herself.

So far so good. But if there's one thing I learned from Mom's weddings it's this: Keep the action moving along. It's only a matter of minutes before these girls start sword fighting with their fans or using them to scoop up the dip. I had really, really wanted to wait for Mom to witness this part, but I have no idea what's keeping her or how much longer it will take. I wink once with each eye to signal Lauren and she beelines around the corner. I wait for it.

And wait for it.

And wait for it.

Finally, I gather my long skirt in my hands and slide

past the partygoers and around the corner. I spot the problem immediately.

Lauren is standing in the doorway, whisper-yelling Becca's name into the house.

"*What* are you doing?" I ask.

"I'm calling for Becca." She sounds so matter-of-fact.

"But she's not there. Why don't you go inside and find her?"

Lauren's eyes go wide. "I *told you*. I am *not* setting foot in there."

"Oh for the love of peccadilloes, Lo." I squeeze past her and into the sunny hallway. Honestly, there is nothing at all scary about—

BANG!

I scream and jump through the doorway, landing on top of Lauren on the floor of the porch. Around the corner, the entire party erupts in gasps and screams.

Before I can react, Vi goes tearing past me, her flip-flops snapping against the wooden floor and her hand to her forehead. "Heavens, y'all! Miss Rebecca has been shot! Murdered!"

The guests look from one to another, and then their open mouths turn up at the corners as they catch on that this is part of the entertainment. Which, I mean, obviously, I knew too. It was just that I didn't expect the shot from the cap gun I brought to be so loud. Or to happen just then. My heart thuds back to normal speed and I roll off Lauren as Vi keeps on with her role.

"Okay, ladies. It's up to us to solve this murder! If you reach under your seats, you'll find an envelope taped to it. Inside will be a description of your role and any information your character has about the suspects," Vi says.

Lauren is back on her feet now too and she starts handing out tiny notepads and pens so our detectives can write down clues if they need to. My heart swells a little bit as I realize we really did think of everything.

The girls are giggling and introducing themselves to their friends with their new names, which all begin with "Miss." Lauren wrote them each specific roles as debutantes attending a cotillion ball at the plantation. As one, they move into the foyer of the house, where the "body" of Becca—er, Miss Rebecca—lies sprawled. Wow, she's really good at keeping perfectly still. I don't think I've ever seen Becca not in motion—the girl's like a hummingbird. I catch Vi's eye and we grin at each other.

Ryan jumps right into his role too, like he's had

a month to memorize his lines off the script Lauren wrote. "Oh no, not Miss Rebecca! My betrothed. And I was so looking forward to our wedding next month."

"You were not, big brother!" Molly, aka the birthday girl, accuses. "You told me this morning that you think she's too bossy for you!"

Ha! I bet Becca's twitching inside at that one. The other girls all giggle. YES! Molly's totally nailing her lines and she didn't have anything more than her note card to go off of. Vi and I high-five—well, more like low-five—behind our skirts.

Mrs. Campbell says, "Well, I have to say, now that Miss Rebecca is gone, perhaps this will clear the way for my Miss Samantha to have a chance with the groom-to-be," and I feel like things are going well enough that I can sneak out of the foyer and into the kitchen to check on the cake. Vi's right behind me.

Or she was.

"Vi?" I peek back into the hallway from the kitchen.

She's standing in front of the enormous grandfather clock, her head tilted just a bit and this teeny-tiny smile on her face. If this wasn't Vi, I'd say she was checking out her reflection in the glass.

"Vi!" I say a little louder.

"Sorry! I was just . . . checking the time." Her face turns red as she flip-flops down the hallway to the kitchen. "So, um, did you notice where Lauren got to? You'd think she'd want to see her play in action."

I poke my head out the back door and, sure enough, Lauren is bustling around the porch, cleaning off the tables and resetting them for the dessert course. "For someone soooo mature for her age, she is seriously the biggest baby ever when it comes to *not*-haunted houses." I say it extra loud so my voice carries over the porch. Lauren glances up and sticks her tongue out at me. I duck back into the kitchen, only to find Vi standing completely frozen, gazing at the cake.

"What's up?" I look back and forth between her and the cake.

She points at the cake. "That bratty, stuck-up, princess-wannabe, good-for-nothing—"

"Vi, *what*?" I ask.

"That is *not* Rhett and Scarlett."

I follow her finger to the tiny couple on the frosting "lawn" of the plantation replica cake. Uh-oh.

It's a tiny hobo with a handkerchief parcel slung over his shoulder standing next to a miniature Little Orphan Annie. Um . . .

"I'm going to KILL Linney," Vi says.

"Uh, Vi, so I know Linney's a total snob and all, and y'all have *history*, but what exactly did you ask for when you placed the order?"

"I *asked* for Rhett and Scarlett." Vi's voice is a little squeaky and she starts pacing the kitchen, which would be funny since it makes her skirt get all tangled up every time she pivots but obviously isn't funny because she's seriously mad.

"And she said they had them?" I had actually been a little surprised they happened to have figurines of Rhett and Scarlett in stock.

Vi stops pacing and starts twisting a napkin she grabs off the counter. She avoids looking at me. "Well, I, um, I'm *pretty sure* Linney said she had them. I guess I was in such a hurry to get away from that monster that I might not have been paying attention to her answer. But I *thought* she said she had them. I'm calling the bakery."

Vi fumbles around in her skirt, trying to find the opening to her pocket, while I calmly remove the Annie and hobo figures from the top layer of the cake. As she dials, I duck back outside and snag a flower vase Lauren is lifting up as she brushes crumbs from the tablecloth.

"I need to borrow this for a sec," I tell her.

I can hear Vi on the phone in the kitchen talking to Linney. "Seriously? You had to *know* Orphan Annie would not be an okay replacement for Scarlett. What do you mean, she's supposed to be me? I don't even have red hair! And for your information, both my parents are *alive*. My mom's just not . . . here. And what, is the hobo supposed to be my dad? Because that's just . . ."

I brush past Vi and grab the phone out of her hand, hitting end on the call. I pass it back to her and calmly arrange flowers in a delicate pattern to cover up the divots in the frosting lawn.

"It's totally fine, Vi. Look!"

I step back and admire my work while Vi continues to jam her thumb on the end-call button about fifty times. She gives me a tight smile and spares one little look at the cake. "It looks beautiful. Nice save. But this is *not* fine. When I see that girl—"

From the foyer, someone shouts, "You did it, Miss Molly! *You* killed Miss Rebecca!" I rush back to the guests to find Molly taking a ginormous bow. She's grinning ear to ear as she leans over and helps the formerly dead Miss Rebecca to her feet. Everyone applauds (Mrs. Campbell hardest of all).

"Forgive me for shooting you?" Molly asks, and

Becca hugs her. Then Becca reaches back and tries to pull Ryan into the circle. He joins them and takes a bow too, but I notice he drops Becca's hand the second he straightens back up. She looks as if she'd like to play dead again, but she shakes it off pretty well.

We all file back out onto the porch where Vi and Lauren are rolling the cart with the cake into place beside the guest of honor's chair.

"Best party EVER," Molly says to her mom, who turns to me with a giant smile on her face.

It totally is. Except for the fact that *my* guest of honor, and the one person I was most trying to impress today, was a complete and total no-show.

What now?

6

Lauren

scheme noun \ˈskēm\
an official plan of action
Use in a sentence:
I have a scheme to get into a really good college
(unlike certain brothers): study hard, save lots of
money, ace the SAT, and do lots of extracurriculars.

I squint at the tiny numbers on the phone screen that
show my savings account total. Seriously, $1,252.16?
That's *it*? That would pay for, what, three days at college? Saving money is so much harder than I thought
it would be. Even after I deposit my share of last
night's party earnings, my total will still look kind of
pathetic.

Of course, it would help if I actually had some

money to save, besides the pittance Dad gives me to work at the marina. Pittance: a small portion, wage, or allowance. Memorized that one after the party last night. I read somewhere that the only way to really remember new words is to use them in sentences. Even if it drives your friends crazy.

My stomach growls, and I log out of my bank account to go in search of food. It's super quiet in my house today. Mom got called into the hospital to do an emergency surgery, Dad dragged Zach to work at the marina, and Josh is at college, taking summer classes to try to fix the GPA he messed up last semester. It's the perfect day to dig into some of the math practice questions for my SAT study class.

I trip over one of Zach's size 95ish Nikes on the way to the kitchen. But it's so worth it, because I have leftover PB&J from yesterday's party just waiting for me in the fridge. I'd scrawled LAUREN'S—TOUCH IT AND DIE on the foil wrapping covering the plate, and shoved the whole thing in the back.

I set my phone on the sailboat-patterned countertop and open the fridge. Who knows where anyone even buys a boat-patterned countertop, but trust my dad to have found the one place that does. There in the back—right where I left it—is the plate of PB&J.

Under the wrapping is one quarter of a delicate crustless sandwich.

One quarter.

"Zach!" I yell, even though there's no way he can hear me from the marina. I even *gave* him a couple of the sandwiches last night, out of the kindness of my sisterly heart.

I'm deciding whether I want to eat the little PB&J or shove it into one of his shoes when my phone sounds the Batman theme, immediately followed by a line from a rap song.

Sadie. And my grandmother, Bubby.

I take a bite and read Bubby's message first, since I'm pretty sure I know what Sadie's says.

Know where I can borrow a dog? I don't even want to know what that's about.

No . . . why? I type back, against my better judgment.

New McDreamy @ Sr Living. Has a pug. Want to impress him with my love of dogs. Sometimes I wonder if Bubby is really my grandma, or actually Becca's. Although I guess I know exactly how Dad got so weird.

Will let you know if I find a spare dog, I reply.

I click over to Sadie's message as I stuff the last of the sandwich into my mouth. It's the Bat Signal. She probably wants to debrief us on what happened with her mom last night. I can't believe Mrs. Pleffer never showed. At least one of my parents shows up to every last thing I do, even if it's just holding down a chair as our school's It's All Academic team alternate. Or maybe they're just happy that one of their kids actually cares about school.

Finding a spot for the sandwich plate in the dishwasher is not exactly easy, but I shove it in there before scrawling a note to Mom. I dash upstairs, pull my latest shell finds from my backpack, and replace them with my SAT math workbook just in case everyone's running late. Then I sprint to the door.

Envelopes are piled up in the little boat-shaped basket under the mail slot. I flip through them, even though I hardly ever get any for myself. The only interesting thing today is a letter from Raleigh State University, addressed to Mom and Dad. I hold it up to the light coming from the brass ship's lantern on an end table. I can't see through the envelope, but I'm pretty sure it's another note threatening to kick Josh out of school.

I kind of want to hide it because Mom cries every time she gets one of these letters. My brothers are absolutely useless. I mean, how do you get almost kicked out of the biggest party school in the state? And it's not like Zach is going to do any better. When I'm in some big-name school in Massachusetts or New York (because all those big-name schools seem to be in Massachusetts or New York), studying to be a general surgeon just like Mom, they'll never get letters like this.

Which is why I need to save up tons of money and get scholarships. Mom makes enough to pay bills and afford state college tuition, but definitely not enough for the kind of college I want to go to. And Dad just barely keeps the marina afloat (pun definitely intended). As Bubby likes to say, the boat business is a sinking business.

I toss the envelope back into the basket. Taped to the door is a note from Mom.

Lauren Phoebe Simmons—Do NOT forget to water the plants. Outside and inside.
Love, Mom

I pull the note off and stuff it into my pocket. I'll water them the second I get back. You'd think Mom would realize by now that I don't need notes with my full name on them to remember to do things. But I guess it's hard to get out of the habit when your oldest kids are Josh and Zach. I think she and Dad expect me to wake up one day as a girl version of my brothers.

I read Question 1 in my math workbook as I start the golf cart parked in the garage. Just because I'm driving a golf cart doesn't mean I can't solve for x in my head. Dad bought a couple of these things to get around the marina, and I'd been dying to drive one for years. The town ordinances say you have to be twelve in order to operate a golf cart on the streets. Which makes no sense, because I wasn't magically more responsible on my January 8 birthday than I was on January 7. Anyway, Mom went on and on about golf-cart crashes and concussions and spiral fractures, but Dad finally convinced her that if anyone would drive a golf cart safely, it'd be me. I'm just not allowed to drive with any of my friends in the cart. Or go on Coastline Drive, because Mom says everyone drives like a maniac on that road.

By the time I roll into the marina, I have the math problem solved. I stop next to the office, knock on the window to wave to Dad and Zach, and then drive on toward the *Purple People Eater*.

Vi's lounging in a small patch of shade on the deck of the yacht. Her nose is bright red.

"What happened?" I ask as I park the cart.

"To what?"

"Your nose, Rudolph." I unlock the door to the *PPE* and we move down the dark steps to the Bat Cave.

"I was out all morning swimming, and then I fell asleep on the beach. Forgot to put on more sunblock. Hey, where'd all that warm water go?" Vi opens cabinet doors as I crack the windows and round up the basket of flashlights.

I point with a flashlight to the little bar in the far corner of the cabin. Vi snags a bottle just as Sadie and Becca arrive. We all sit around the flashlight basket— all of us except Becca, who's just standing there in her bright white sundress.

"What are you doing?" Sadie asks her.

"I don't want to get old yacht dirt on my dress," she says. "Sorry, Lo."

Like I'm going to be offended about the state of the *Purple People Eater*. I empty out my backpack and pass it to Becca. "Here, sit on this."

She sits super gently on the backpack, as if the very act of sitting will make dirt seep into her dress.

"So did you find out why your mom didn't come to the party?" Vi asks Sadie.

Sadie makes a face. "She said she felt really bad about it, but she had a bridezilla freaking out and she had to drop everything and meet with her and I wasn't answering my cell. I had it on vibrate so it wouldn't interrupt the party. Whatever."

Sadie gives a little shake of her head. "I mean, not whatever, but what can I do? I guess it's partly my fault because I was trying to surprise her, so I didn't tell her what it was she was coming to and she didn't realize it was a one-time-only thing she was missing out on. Anyway, my mom's not why I sent the Bat Signal. Not totally, anyway."

"Wait, did you change your mind and now you're going to help me get Ryan's attention?" Becca looks like someone's given her an all-expenses-paid trip to Hawaii. "Because I have the perfect idea—"

"No, not that." Sadie's biting her lip, probably to

avoid telling Becca how hard Ryan worked to steer clear of her at the party.

We all look at her, waiting for an explanation.

"Well . . . ," Sadie finally says. "I have this idea. It sort of has to do with the 'one-time-only thing' I mentioned. Hear me out before you say no. So, you know how none of us have any real summer plans?"

Speak for yourself. My brain is already sorting out my summer schedule.

"I have plans," Becca says. "Ryan plans. You want to hear them?"

"No," we all say together.

"What's your idea, Sades?" Vi asks, chin on her knees. Vi'd been hoping to go to this amazing soccer camp in Charlotte for a couple weeks this summer, but the price was pretty amazing too.

"Well . . . I think we should start a business," Sadie says.

"Doing what?" I ask.

"What do you mean, doing what? Party planning!" Sadie's grinning now. "We totally rocked it at Molly's party. Mrs. Campbell was so happy, she even asked if we had business cards, because she wanted to recommend us to her friends!"

"I'm not sure," I say. "With all of my stuff, and

Vi's sports, and Becca's . . . boyfriend search." Becca elbows me.

"It's summer! We all have plenty of time," Sadie says. "Besides, just think about how much fun it would be." Sadie's phone rings in her hand. She glances down at the screen and hits ignore.

"Your mom?" I ask.

"Nah, just my sister. Okay, so where was I? Becca, you could drum up business, since you know everyone in town. And you could convince that Ryan guy to help us out sometimes, right?"

Becca sits up straighter and suddenly looks a thousand percent more interested in this business idea.

"Vi could cook some—" Sadie starts to say.

"No way," Vi says as she twists the ends of her ponytail. "What if I mess it up?"

"Impossible," I tell her.

"And, Lauren, you'd be a whiz at making sure we stay on budget for each party."

I shake my head. "I wish I could, but I *really* don't have the time."

"And the money!" Sadie goes on like she hasn't even heard me. "Just think of how much money we could make. If we book one party per week, and maybe even book two parties once in a while, and we have how many weeks till school starts again?"

Everyone looks at me.

"Eight," I fill in. Eight weeks of SAT study so I can take a practice test in September. Eight weeks of racking up enough volunteer hours to be considered for the school volunteer award. Eight weeks of listening to Bubby go on and on about the newest eligible eighty-year-old to move into her complex. Eight weeks of marina work to try to boost my bank account. Eight weeks, eight weeks, eight weeks.

"So that's somewhere between eight and sixteen parties, so we could earn—"

"A lot of money," Vi chimes in. She's stopped twisting her ponytail and is smiling. I know she's thinking about that kayak for her dad. She only stops to look at it every day. "I'm in."

"Becca?" Sadie asks.

"Yes . . . *if* I can bring Ryan. You know how he's dying to practice his acting skills or whatever. He won't be able to say no to this!" She grins at us like she expects us to be jumping up and down. "Oh, don't give me that look. You know we'll need a boy for some of these parties."

"Fine. But we're only paying him if he's actually needed," Sadie says. "So . . . Lauren?"

Ugh, I hate saying no to my friends. Especially to Sadie. They're all looking at me so expectantly. And I feel really, really selfish. Maybe if I moved my volunteer work to Wednesday and stayed up a little later to study . . .

"Remember how you gave me that shell and told me I was on a new journey? Well, maybe you are too," Sadie says.

Sadie knows me way too well. Of course, I know her just as well, and I definitely know when she's bringing everything she has to convince me. And I'd give in too, if I didn't have this SAT class. There's no way I can move everything around or stay up later and still get it all done. Selfish or not, I've already committed to all this stuff. People expect me to show up and to be perfect.

"Sades, I—"

Sadie looks right at me. "Lauren, did you or did you not have fun on Saturday?"

I nod.

"Did you like writing that script for the murder mystery?"

"Yes." That was the best part. It was nice writing something that wasn't due for a class.

"Y'all know how crazy busy I am with swimming and volleyball and surfing," Vi says, her red nose shining in the flashlight's glow. "But I'm thinking, even though this party idea will take time away from all that, it's something we can do together. And it's fun!"

"You need some fun," Becca says to me. The super-serious look on her face almost makes me laugh. It's like she's holding a fun-intervention for her study-addicted friend.

"Just think of all the different kinds of parties we can come up with. And then make them happen—together!" Forget the flashlights, Sadie's smile could light up the room on its own.

"And we can make moolah, cash, dough, scratch, MON-EY!" Becca says, rubbing her hands together like some cartoon villain. She's probably thinking about some skirt or pair of shoes her parents refuse to buy for her.

I pinch the bridge of my nose. "Will y'all stop ganging up on me? I said I can't do it. I'd explode from all the stress."

"But it won't be the same without you," Sadie says.

She's completely guilting me. And it's so hard to say no, especially when I really want to say yes. "Look, I'll help you set it up. Make a business plan and all that. But really, that's all I can do."

Sadie's smile falters a bit, and a few tears leak out of her eyes.

"Wait, why are you crying?" Becca asks.

"Did I make you cry?" Now I feel really awful. What kind of friend am I?

"No. But I'm not giving up on you yet, Lauren. I'm crying because I'm so, so, SO happy!" Sadie says through her tears. "We'll plan so many parties, the law of averages means my mom will have to make at least *one* of them. But that's totally a bonus. Really, I'm just psyched to have the best friends in the world."

Except Lauren. Sadie doesn't say that, of course, but I still feel like the most horrible, selfish best friend in the world. I don't have a choice, though. Future Lauren would not be okay with Right Now Lauren if I blew off my responsibilities to hang out with my friends and then didn't get into Cornell or Harvard.

But somehow that still doesn't make me feel better.

"Lauren!" Becca's waving at me. They're all leaned into one big, squishy *Purple People Eater* hug. I join them, wrapping my arms around Becca and Sadie, and putting on a pretend smile like some sort of fake friend.

"Now let's get down to business." Sadie scrubs the tears from her face with the back of her hand.

"What did you say you were going to write, Lauren? Business stuff?" Vi asks.

I fumble through the mess on the floor and find a notebook and my lucky test-taking pen. The least I can do is help them get this started the right way. I really want to write *Business Stuff* at the top, but that's super unprofessional. Even if I'm not an official part of the business, I want to make it look the best I can for my friends. After an hour, we have something like a plan written out.

Party-Planning Business
Company Owners: Sadie Pfeffer,
Violet Alberhasky, Rebecca Elldridge

"No one calls me Violet," Vi says as I read the page out loud.

"This is a business plan," I inform her. "You have to use your full name."

"No," she says as she lunges for my pen.

"Okay, fine!" I cross out the *-olet* from her name.

Goal: To plan parties for kids (or anyone who wants to hire us).

"Except sixth-grade boys. They're way too immature," Becca says.

"I'm not writing that down," I say as I tap the notebook with my slim black pen.

Benefits for customers: We handle all the planning, book the venue, get the cake and food, book entertainment, buy party favors, send out invitations, and clean up afterward.

"Can't we hire someone to clean up?" Becca asks. "Picking up all those chips from the porch of the Poinsettia Plantation was a nightmare."

"Not if we want to keep the money we make," Sadie says.

Tasks: Will be split evenly among all business owners. If someone can't get something done, she needs to tell the others right away.

Cost: Depends on the party. Simple parties will cost less than extravagant parties. Cost will include cake, party favors, food, etc., and that part will be paid up front because we don't have any money.

"Whatever, Miss Moneybags." Vi elbows me.

"I'm not a part of this, remember? And besides, that's for college."

Transportation: Bike.

"What if something's really far away?" Vi asks.

Becca shoots me an innocent grin. "I think Lauren should drive us in that golf cart."

"For the ninetieth time, I'm not in the business. And I can't drive the cart with anyone else in it. You know that." Becca's only begged me at least once a week since January to take her somewhere in the golf cart.

"My mom is way too busy to drive us anywhere," Sadie says as she pushes dirt around the floor with her finger.

"And my dad works all the time," Vi says.

I throw my arms up. "Okay, fine. If you're really desperate—and I mean really, intensely desperate—I can guilt Zach into driving you somewhere. But you might regret it. Remember how much he complained just taking us to the Plantation House? And he's a really awful driver."

Advertising: Get parents to make copies
of flyers and put them up everywhere.
Order free business cards online.

Officers:

"I nominate Sades for President," Vi says.

"Seconded," Becca says.

"Since Becs got that party with Mrs. Campbell, maybe she should be in charge of booking parties and advertising?" Vi tightens her ponytail and looks like she wants to say something else. "But, um . . . what does that leave for me?"

I study the paper in front of me. "A treasurer. You need someone to take care of the money. And probably someone to take notes at any business meetings."

"I know someone who'd be perfect for that," Becca says in a singsong voice. She flutters her eyelashes at me and that guilty feeling pinches my stomach again.

"No, already. Not me. It has to be Vi." I add another line to the business plan.

Sadie—President, Vi—secretary/Treasurer, Becca—Booking/Advertising

"How about 'Queen of Booking and Advertising'?" Becca smooths her straight red hair like she's ready for us to pop a tiara on it.

"This is a democracy," Sadie says. "No queens allowed."

I set the notebook next to the flashlight basket, and we all lean in to admire it.

"We need a name," Becca says. "Parties 4 U?"

"Plethora of Parties?" I suggest. Then I clamp my mouth shut. This isn't my business.

"What does 'plethora' mean?" Vi asks. "How about BVS Parties, or SBV Parties? You know, our initials?"

Becca giggles. "Those sound like diseases. We should do something less obvious."

"Wait." I run Vi's disease names though my head again. There's something there if I use Rebecca instead of Becca. "RSVP!"

"RS—what?" Vi blinks at me.

"RSVP. *Répondez s'il vous plaît*. Please respond," I translate. "The fancy-schmancy French way of saying 'Hey, can you make it or not?'"

"It's on the bottom of every invitation. RSVP." Sadie says the word like she's testing it out. "It's kind of . . . perfect."

"And get this: R for Rebecca, S for Sadie, V for Vi, and P for . . . whatever," I add.

"We should change it to RSVL. Then you'd have to join because your name is in there." Becca gives me this sneaky smile.

"Yeah, no." It's not as if I can change the French language. Also, it's like a sign. My name doesn't fit when everyone else's does, so obviously it's the universe telling me that I need to concentrate on everything else I already have lined up this summer. Not that signs are really a thing. But if I did believe in them, this would definitely be one, and who am I to argue with the universe?

I hold the pen over the notebook. "So, RSVP?"

"That's perfect." Vi unfolds her long legs and leans forward in a stretch.

"Very classy," Becca adds.

Sadie brushes her bangs out of her eyes and smiles. "RSVP it is."

I add the name to the top of our business plan. I mean, *their* business plan.

Becca's phone buzzes and she groans. "It's Dad," she says. "My presence is required at the Visitor's Center tomorrow. I'm supposed to fill in as the guide for the walking tours."

"What happened to Pete?" I ask.

"Said he needed to clear out of town before the Fourth of July crowds descend on us." She stands up and brushes imaginary flecks of dirt from her dress. "Better enjoy my freedom today, then."

"Wait, y'all should figure out who's doing what first." I write down all of their names under the words *Action Plan*.

"I'll make some flyers and ask Mom how to order business cards. And we can pass out the flyers at the Fourth of July parade and cookout next weekend," Becca says as she hands me my backpack.

"I'll . . . um . . . well, there's no money yet, and everything we talked about is in that business plan," Vi says. "Wait, I know! I'll make a spreadsheet so we can track all the money we earn."

A spreadsheet. I could whip that up in two minutes flat. Two minutes that would be better spent memorizing another vocab word definition, I have to remind myself. I tear the business plan from my notebook and pass it to Sadie.

Sadie carefully folds the pages and stows them in her purse. "I'll put together some planning worksheets so that they're ready to go once we book a party."

I cap my pen and load everything back into my backpack. Then we climb the steps, and I lock up the *Purple People Eater*.

"To RSVP!" Becca says. "This is going to be so much fun!" She holds up her hand. Vi and Sadie do the same—a group high-five. I look away because it hurts just a teeny-tiny bit that I've taken myself out of the group like this. It would've been kind of nice if my name happened to be Patricia or Pam or Petunia. Okay, maybe not Petunia. But maybe if the sign had been there, I could've moved some things around. Maybe.

My phone belts out a rap song. It's a text from Bubby.

Party on, Lo baby!

How Bubby already knows about RSVP, I don't know. But I can already imagine how disappointed she'll be when I tell her I'm not part of it.

"And we're going to make tons of money," Vi says as the four of us walk down the dock. "We could make more than your mom, Sades."

Sadie smiles, and Vi gives her a sideways hug.

"Maybe we can do another play like we did for Molly's party, but this time I could take the role of Ryan's girlfriend," Becca says.

Vi rolls her eyes. "I wonder if we should set up some kind of taste-testing with caterers? Like what Sadie's mom does for the brides. So, you know, we'll learn about who's the best."

"I know who'd be the best," Becca says. "You."

"Just think of all the trips we'll get to make to Party Me Hearties." Sadie has this far-off look in her eyes, like Party Me Hearties is the Six Flags of Sandpiper Beach instead of this sprawling party supplies store on the mainland with bad lighting and cranky salespeople.

"This is going to be the best summer ever!" Becca says.

I can't stand Party Me Hearties (I mean, that name. Really.) and want to die at the thought of having to be in a silly murder-mystery play. But . . . there's something kind of lonely about walking behind my friends as they go on and on about this stuff. They don't even look back at me as I climb into the parked golf cart. It's almost like I've gone from best friend to fake friend to nobody in an hour.

I try to imagine my college savings account skyrocketing as I put in hours at the marina and the size of the scholarships I'll get when I ace the SAT. Not to mention my parents' faces when I do all of that. It'll totally make up for everything Josh and Zach haven't done. And it won't make for such a bad summer, right?

If I ignore the little twinge in my heart when I think of my best friends having fun without me.

7

Becca

Daily Love Horoscope for Scorpio:
Keep your friends close today, and your
enemies even closer.

*H*istory with swishy Southern belles and romantic old plantation houses? Yes, please. History about the so-small-it's-majorly-a-miracle-we-have-our-own-zip-code town, where I've lived my *entire* life? Snore, snore, snoozefest.

At least Daddy's not making me dress up in the pirate costume to give the walking tour this time because, take it from me, horizontal stripes are exactly *no one's* friend. And that stuffed parrot I'm supposed to wear on my shoulder has the sharpest fake claws I've *ever* encountered. Okay, well, not like I've encountered a bazillion fake claws or anything, but one set is more than enough, thankyouverymuch.

I zoom my bike through the open double doors of the Visitor's Center and right behind the counter, even though I know this will make Daddy especially crazy. But he's forcing me to give this tour—again—so I kind of can't help getting back at him just a little bit.

"I'm here," I announce.

"Yes, I can see that," Daddy says, not even commenting on the super-clunky handlebars that will probably hit him in the butt every time he needs to get someone change for the souvenir penny machine. He barely even gives them a passing glance when he says, "Oh, and by the way, I changed my mind about the pirate costume."

Um, say what now?

"*Daaaaddy!* That's so not fair. You can't do that!"

"Well, Rebecca, if you can feel free to take liberties with agreements we've made in the past"—he pauses and points his eyes directly at my beach cruiser behind the counter—"then I think it's perfectly *fair* for me to back down on my word as well."

Then he shrugs and smiles as if he doesn't have a care in the whole wide world. Can you imagine? My hands go to my hips and I open my mouth to argue back, but he slides out from behind the counter and approaches a woman studying a brochure for the fudge shop up the street.

"They offer free samples and a live fudge-making demonstration on the half hour," Daddy tells her, motioning behind his back for me to go to the store-room where the Dread Pirate Roberts costume lives. Sadie named it that when she was in her *Princess Bride* obsession stage. Ha! The dread part is definitely spot-on. As in, I *dread* the thought of putting this costume on.

I consider mutiny, but who even knows what punishment Daddy would cook up for me then. He might actually make me walk the plank on the sunset cruise or something. And I don't want to think about what salt water would do to my hair.

Sighing as loudly as I possibly can, I trudge off to the storage closet and grab the musty costume and stuffed Polly Want a Cracker. Five minutes later, I step out of the bathroom behind the Visitor's Center, fully costumed. I tug at the pleather pants. Even though they're, like, approximately one hundred and twenty-two sizes too big for me, they're already glued by sweat to my thighs. The fact that they're tucked into even stickier pleather boots does *not* help. It should be against the law to wear fake leather in North Carolina in June. (Or anywhere ever, actually.)

Ugh.

It's not even a semicool pirate costume with a hook or a peg leg or anything. Instead of Captain Hook, I look more like Smee with my red-and-white-striped shirt and the bandanna around my head. I'm so getting back at my dad for this. Just wait until he wants me to play a guitar duet with him at our next beach bonfire.

"You look darling, my darling," Mama calls, balancing two iced coffees in a carryout tray on her hip and heading toward me from across the square. "It's not like you to be early. If I'd known, I would have grabbed you a sweet tea on my drink run. Let me drop this coffee with your dad and I'll be right back."

A minute later, while I contemplate cutting air pockets into my pants, she's in front of me again. "How was your morning?"

"Fine." I can't help it if I grumble when I say it. Mama and Daddy had date night on the mainland last night, so I didn't get to see them, and ordinarily I would be telling Mama all about RSVP, including the gazillion ideas I thought of for drumming up business. Or the flyers I designed last night. I just know she'll let us use the center's copy machine for them. But I'm too sticky and pirate-y to get excited about *anything*.

Mama sets her drink down on a bench and adjusts Polly on my shoulder. "There. She was crooked."

Le sigh.

"Your tour is meeting over by Merlin in five. Want me to walk with you?" Mama asks.

"Nooooo." I drag out the word and droop my head. Why doesn't anyone care that I'm positively melting in this costume? I manage a halfhearted wave good-bye before shuffling across the square to the brass statue of Merlin, the biggest Atlantic marlin ever recorded, weighing an astounding 1,576 pounds. Caught in 1942 by the great-great-plus-a-zillion-more-greats-grandson of town founder Jebediah Bodington. Just another uber-fascinating statistic, courtesy of Lauren's fact-checking. (Seriously, her favorite thing to do is take the tour and correct my dad when he says there were 120 settlers aboard the *Rosalinde* instead of 121.) And now the friendly visitors to Sandpiper Beach will learn all about them on their informative and entertaining walking tour today. Yippy skippy.

Which reminds me—time for my hourly text to Lauren. In addition to Operation Get a Boyfriend, I'm also on Operation Get Lauren to Join RSVP. I figure if I annoy her enough, she'll give in. And what's more annoying than your BFF texting you every single hour—even at night? When my alarm went off at three a.m., I sent her a text that said, "Lo, join us or ghoisdgihskd," because my fingers hit the wrong buttons and I was too asleep to really notice. But whatever. I got my point across.

Merlin says u have 2 join RSVP. Or he'll find u & give u smooshy slobbery fish kisses. I hit send.

No response. When I started my campaign yesterday afternoon, she'd protest after every text I sent and say she couldn't join because of the STAs or whatever. Then she just sent texts that said, Shut up, B. :) Today she hasn't responded at all.

I'm totally wearing her down.

I stuff my phone somewhere in the costume. I'll probably never find it again. No one's here yet. It's just me and good ol' Merlin. It's not like I'd ever admit this out loud or anything, but sometimes I bounce song ideas off of the fishy-face marlin, and I'm thinking that might be exactly the thing to snap me out of my funk when

Mrs. O'Malley rounds the other side of the brass fish.

"Oh, Rebecca, it's you. I rather hoped we'd have Pete for today's tour."

Um, hello. Rude much? And what's cranky old Mrs. O'Malley doing taking a tour meant for visi— Wait, wait, wait. Did she say "we"?

Mrs. O'Malley's face breaks into a smile at the sight of someone behind me and I whirl around to spot Ryan crossing the square in our direction, a dripping ice-cream cone in one hand.

Bye-bye, funk!

When he sees me next to Mrs. O'Malley, he trips a little on one of the cobblestones. Omigosh, omigosh omigosh. Do I make him nervous? *Eep!*

Orrrrr, it could be the Ahoy-there-mateys look I'm rocking. I shiver (me timbers) even though it's June. In North Carolina.

Well, whatever. I can't help how I'm dressed. I'm just going to have to wow him with my sparkling per-sonality instead. I turn a giant smile on Mrs. O'Malley. "I'm so glad you're taking the tour today, ma'am."

She looks a lot surprised. What? It's not like I've never called her "ma'am" before. Probably.

"Well, Rebecca, I thought it might be good for

my great-nephew to have a sense of the history of our little town, seeing as he'll be spending the summer with us."

With *us*. Yes, please.

Ryan arrives at my side and I beam up at him. His smile seems more polite than friendly, but I'll bet it's just because he doesn't want to flirt in front of his great-aunt. Which is *soo* thoughtful of him. I totally respect that.

"Nice parrot," he says.

Nice parrot. Omigosh, could he be any cuter and wittier? I am going to make such beautiful music out of our relationship. Obviously, it will include a verse with "Nice Parrot." What rhymes with "parrot"? "Wear it?" "Spare it?" "Carrot?"

Polly's claws don't seem nearly as razor-bladey as they did a minute ago. In fact, I can barely feel them. Let's get this tour STARTED!

Mrs. O'Malley tells Ryan the story of Merlin the fish, and I don't even correct her when she gets the date *and* the name of the fisherman who caught him slightly wrong. Lauren could learn a thing or two from me. If Ryan can be respectful of his elders, so can I.

A family with sleeping toddler twins in a stroller join us, and then a stylish woman with a scarf and a sketchpad shows up and says my dad told her to tell me she was the last of the group.

"Okay then!" I say with newfound enthusiasm. "We're off." I slip one arm through Mrs. O'Malley's and try to loop my other through Ryan's, but he backs away just before I reach him. I think he might be scared of Polly Want a Cracker.

I lead the way from the town square to the public beach access so I can show my group the tip-top part of a shipwreck poking out between waves a little way offshore. We've had to restore the wood on the mast a few times, so it's probably not technically historical anymore, but the tourists don't have to know that.

"See that? It's the top of a sunken clipper ship from the 1800s. This part of North Carolina's coastline is called the Graveyard of the Atlantic because we have as many as three thousand shipwrecks between here and Kitty Hawk. There are all these sandbars underwater that no one could ever map because they were constantly moving with the tides, and plus we get lots of hurricanes in this part of the country. So tons and tons of crashed ships and, like, buried treasure."

Out of the corner of my eye, I notice that Ryan

perks up a little at this, so I decide to work that angle.

"Oh and also," I say, "we used to have loads of pirates around here. Up in Nags Head, there were even land pirates. So what they did was"—I pause to make sure everyone (*cough* Ryan *cough*) is paying attention— "they hung a light around a horse's neck and then put the nag on the beach so when she moved it looked sort of like a ship's lantern bobbing around. And the captains would steer their ships close to check out the other ship and then *BAM!*"

Ryan jumps back a little. Whoops. Might have cranked up the enthusiasm a wee bit too much there.

I dial it down on my volume and softly say, "They would get stuck in the sandbars and the land pirates would wade out and board their ships and take everything back to shore. Cool, huh?"

The parents of the twins look impressed, but Ryan just shrugs and jams his hands in the pockets of his shorts. He's wearing that orange drama camp shirt. Again. Not like orange isn't a good color on him, because it totes is, but maybe when I'm his girlfriend I can convince him to branch out just a little.

Everyone else is reading all the historical plaques along

the big pavilion next to the boardwalk over the dunes, so I figure it's as good a time as any to grab a little one-on-one time with the inspiration for my future hit single.

"You look kind of bored. Are you, like, not a fan of pirates or something?" I ask.

"They're okay. Although it's kind of funny to hear the 1800s described as ancient history. Some of our historical sites are older than the pyramids. I guess America's kind of a baby when you compare it to Ireland."

Pfft. Whatever. Land pirates for the win. But, I mean, it's not like I care enough to fight with Ryan over it, especially since he's actually sort of smiling at me now.

"I prefer new to old anyway," I tell him. "And speaking of new, I have something you might be interested in. Our new business! Which could mean more acting gigs for you-know-who!"

Ryan perks up a little, before studying me. "What's the catch?"

Oh, no catch. You just have to fall in love with me and be my boyfriend and let me write alllll the songs about you. That won't be a problem, will it?

Obviously, I don't say *that*.

"No catch. We're going to make the party-planning

thing a regular business and we might need someone to help out with the guy roles, that's all."

"By 'we,' do you mean your friends? Vi and Sadie and . . . what's the other girl's name?"

"Lauren. She's not doing it. Well, she *says* she not doing it, but I refuse to accept that. I can be very persuasive when I want to be. I don't take no for an answer easily."

Maybe I should threaten to stuff Polly into her bed if she doesn't join. Now, that would be scary.

Ryan backs one step away, so I take a step toward him as I say, "But Sades and Vi are in. And me, of course."

I flutter my eyelashes like girls are always doing on TV, but he doesn't even notice because at the same time Polly dips forward off my shoulder and dangles by her claws from my shirt. Ergh! So not fair! I cram her back into place while Ryan watches me weirdly.

"Um, I better get back to Aunt Moira. Uh, maybe Vi can fill me in more on the whole party thing at volleyball."

And just like that he walks back to his great-aunt and I swear it's as if she's jelly and he's peanut butter with the way he sticks super close to her the whole rest of the tour. He barely even looks at me, even when one of the twins wakes up and starts shrieking at "the scary, scary pirate." (That would be me, BTW.)

Forget French—this calls for Italian. La sigh! There *have* to be easier ways to land a boyfriend.

And then, just to add insult to . . . well, whatever that saying is . . . right when I'm wrapping up the tour back in the town square, who comes out of the Lava Java with some ridiculous iced coffee drink that probably has a milk-to-coffee ratio of about a thousand to one (I mean, like, who drinks coffee at age *twelve*, even if it *is* mostly milk) but Linney. Blecch.

Of course, Ryan can never know that I'm not always perfectly sweet, sweet, sweet, so when Linney beelines it for me I kind of don't have a choice but to be all friendly and nice.

Except I don't introduce her to Ryan, because nuh-uh. Girlfriend's on her own there. Plus he's over on the bench, scraping something off his shoe while he waits for his great-aunt to use the bathroom.

"So is it true?" Linney asks.

I squint at her. For Linney to pass up the opportunity to make a snide remark about Dread Pirate Roberts is suspicious enough, but for her to think I know something before her is kind of laughable. It's pretty much like she has bugs planted in the walls of every building in town.

"Is what true?" I ask.

"Are you, Sadie, and Violet starting a party-planning business?" Linney asks.

See? Bugs. How else could Linney get her intel so fast?

As if she read my mind, she says, "You tweeted about it yesterday. Obviously."

Oh. So maybe not bugs. But still.

"Um, yeah, I guess it's true." I peek over at Ryan, who is still sitting there, not close enough to be part of the conversation, but not really so far away that he couldn't hear it. Rats, double rats. Still have to be nice.

Linney has a big smile on her face. "Oh, I'm so glad to hear that, because I've just been racking my brains trying to figure out all the details for my Sweet Thirteen, and I sure could use some help."

I let my jaw fall open. Linney wants help from *us*? What is she up to? She's positively up to something. But I glance at Ryan again and swallow the comment that was working its way up to my mouth.

Instead, I say (with my voice oozing sugar), "Don't people usually have Sweet *Sixteen* parties?"

Linney just grins more. "Oh, I'm sure I'll have one of those also."

Blecch again. But I keep smiling too and ask, "What did you have in mind?"

"Well, the theme is *Project Runway*. I was thinking of having my friends decorate plain dresses and then, like, have them accessorize like crazy before we send them down a runway."

Drat. Double drat. TRIPLE drat. Linney just named my dream party and I'll bet she knows it. Of course, *I* could never have that party because Sadie would probably be so busy making lists of what she'd need for her outfit that she'd never actually get around to making one, and Lauren would probably find a way to work math equations into all her hem measurements, and Vi—I stifle a snort. Vi would have to be dragged there kicking and screaming.

Linney is sucking down her iced drink like it's going out of style while she calmly waits for me to respond. What to do? What to do?

On the one hand, it's a party. A real and actual paid party, and my job *is* to go out and find us paid parties, so wouldn't I be completely cuckoo to turn one down that basically fell into our laps? On the other hand, none of us can stand Linney because of the way she treats Vi and because she's, well, so very, very *Linney*.

I open my mouth and then close it again. While I stall, I steal a peek at Ryan and inspiration strikes.

"Hey, Linney. Do you think you'll need an emcee for the runway part? Like someone to tell the audience about the dresses as they come down?"

"Obvs," she answers.

I glance at Ryan again. He would look *ah*-mazing in a tuxedo, announcing the girls as they walked the runway. Then, in my head, I see Vi when I tell her we're doing a party for Linney. It's like there's a devil on one shoulder and an angel on the other, each whispering to me. Oh, wait. There *is* a devil on my shoulder. He just happens to be stuffed and answers to Polly Want a Cracker.

Linney sucks the last remnants of milkfee (that's my new name for it, because you for sure can't get away with calling it coffee) and puts one hand on her hip.

"Look, do y'all want the job or not?"

I know what Polly would say. "Squawk! Take the job! Squawk!"

"We do."

I just hope, hope, hope and pray that Vi forgives me.

FASHION WEEK COMES TO SANDPIPER BEACH!

For stylista VIPs only

You're invited to Linney's Runway,

the haute couture event of the season

Friday, July 10, four o'clock

At the Marks residence, 1115 Live Oak Drive

Come ready to show off your fashion skills and strut

your stuff!

Gifts appreciated. Please see a list of preferred shops at

linneysrunway.com

RSVP to Sadie Pleffer, (910) 555-0110 or

sadie@rsvpmail.com

8

Vi

BACON & ONION SLIDERS

Ingredients:

4 slices bacon

1 onion, chopped

2 cloves garlic, minced

3 lbs lean ground beef

2 tbsp Worcestershire sauce

salt and pepper

small dinner rolls

Cook bacon in a pan, then remove and set on paper towels. When it cools, crumble bacon. Keep 2 tbsp of bacon fat in the pan and use it to cook the onion for 3 minutes. Add the garlic and cook it with the onion for 30 seconds. Combine onion and garlic, ground beef, bacon, Worcestershire sauce, salt, and pepper in a large bowl and mix well. Form mixture into 24 small patties and place in the refrigerator to cool. Cook on a grill or in a pan until cooked through, turning patties as needed. Serve on buns. Optional: add lettuce, cheese, tomato, pickle, avocado, onion, and condiments.

**Dad's favorite, especially when served with Gouda cheese.*

**These are like normal hamburgers dressed up to be tiny and fancy.*

I am going to murder Becca.

No, murder's too nice. First I'm going to throw away all her clothes so she has to wear that Dread Pirate Roberts getup all the time. Then I'm going to make sure that every weekly in town knows how much she just loves getting texts for personal full-day tours of the fish cannery on the mainland. THEN I'm going to tell Ryan that she sleeps with a bald, patched, one-eyed stuffed dog she got when she was four. And after that I'll find out exactly what it is that she writes in that shimmery purple-and-silver notebook and I'll publish it online and send a mass text to everyone in school and—

"Vi?" Sadie's holding out the box of mismatched

high-heeled shoes from Goodwill that are serving as centerpieces for That Monster's party.

I refuse to say the birthday girl's name. Kind of like she's Lord Voldemort.

"When is That Monster getting here?" I smack a mosquito on my arm before taking the box from Sadie. The Markses' house is on the back side of the island, on the Intracoastal Waterway. Which means they have a tiny little dock in their backyard, along with tons of mosquitoes and no-see-ums.

"You know I can't stand her either, but we have to act like professionals. Trust me, Mom and I have worked with some total bridezillas, but you just have to find a way to deal with them. Meaning you have to call Linney by her name."

Sadie climbs up onto the runway she somehow managed to snag from the Sandpiper Beach Daffodil Days Spring Tea Party and Fashion Show and has deposited right here in That Monster's backyard.

"Not a chance." I plop a sequined blue-and-yellow shoe in the middle of That Monster's table of honor. It's probably the ugliest one in the box. And maybe the stinkiest. "Hey, speaking of your mom, did you invite her today?"

"Of course! I filled her in completely this time—no more attempted surprises. I told her everything about RSVP."

"You did?" I add another shoe. It's not quite as ugly as the first one, but it's not pretty either. "What did she say?"

"Well, it's not like I came out and told her it all started so we could prove how worthy I am of getting my job with her back or anything. I told her all the other reasons, like how much fun we were going to have doing it together. She said she thought it was really cute."

Sadie does a little eye roll when she says the word "cute." Then she adds as she jumps down from the runway, "But she'll see. She'll see we're not some kid operation. I can't wait!"

"Me either," I say. "She's going to be so impressed. *If* we get everything set up in time. Not like I want to see her or anything, but just where is The Traitor? She's supposed to be helping us."

"Becca is—"

"Here I am!" The Traitor (formerly known as Becca) wafts through the Markses' pristine white gate with an armload of dresses. "Sorry I'm late. The store was missing two of the sizes we ordered, so I had to wait until *forever* while they searched. Then I saw that it was three o'clock, so I had to send Lo a text telling her that Vi was totally going to mess up the money." Bec—I mean The Traitor—drops the pile on the nearest chair and fans herself.

"What are you talking about? I'm not that bad at numbers." I'm no Lauren, but I pull off solid Bs in math.

"Sorry, but desperate times call for desperate people. Or something. Anyway, OMG, Mama and I passed Ryan on the way over and wait until you see how super cute he looks in a tux. You. Will. DIE! I mean, but not too much, 'cause I saw him first!" She leans against the chair with all the dresses piled on it. The stack teeters for a second and then tumbles from the chair onto the ground. And into the little decorative pond and fountain.

"No! Bec-*ca*!" Sadie's practically wailing.

I drop the box of shoes and race to help pull the dresses from the pond.

"Omigosh, I'm so so so sorry! Look, it's only two of them that got uber-wet. And we still have a half hour before the party starts. *Plennnnnty* of time for them to dry!" She wrings out one of the dresses and then waves it through the air. "See, if I do this, it'll air-dry."

Sadie pinches the bridge of her nose and takes a

deep breath. "Okay, here's what we're going to do. Vi, you take these inside and ask Mrs. Marks if you can put them in the dryer."

"Um, they're dry-clean only," The Traitor says.

"All right. Then, Vi, see if you can borrow a hair dryer and dry them that way. Becs, can you help me get all the accessories and stuff for the dresses out?" Sadie tucks her hair behind her ears. "I really wish Lauren was here. We could use another person to finish the center-pieces and put out the favors and make sure all the guests know to post every picture they take to Linney's—"

"Back up," I say. "You actually want me to go into That Monster's house?"

"Vi . . ." Sadie's wrapping her hair into a ponytail, which for Sadie means she's really getting down to business. "Please? Linney's not even home. I'm going to text Lauren and beg her to come help."

"Fine. And good luck," I grumble as I toss the wet dresses over my arm.

Mrs. Marks is in the kitchen. Sadie said that when she first got here, Mrs. Marks tried to help her set up the tables and stuff, but Linney popped up and pretty much ordered her mom to stay out of our way. So typical for Linney. And get this, she wouldn't even let her mom—the best baker in town—make a cake for the party. Instead, she ordered a bunch of fancy cupcakes from this new café on Main Street, and then she didn't trust any of us to pick them up. Fine with me. Otherwise she'd be out back, making us all insane.

I show Mrs. Marks the dresses, and she waves me on to a bathroom upstairs. The second I step inside, I know it's That Monster's. It's all done up in this cutesy Paris café theme—black-and-white-striped walls, a tiny little pink-cushioned chair with a metal curlicue back, pretty Eiffel Tower doodads all over the place.

So Not Vi. The whole thing makes me feel like an ogre prancing in a ballroom.

I plug in the pink hair dryer and spread the first dress over the countertop. That Monster picked these basic short dresses in a rainbow of colors. The blue is actually sort of pretty, almost like the ocean right before a storm. But the one I'm drying now is a blinding yellow. I aim the dryer with my left hand and pull out my So Not Vi (but still kind of cute) phone with my right to text Lauren. Sadie's right—we definitely need her. Except I need her for more than just pulling off a great party.

Plz come. The Traitor is outside and I'm in That Monster's house. Help.

I can't believe B did that to you. Lauren always knows how to make me feel better. But is prob good for biz, right?

Or not. Seriously, I can't believe how unsupportive my friends are being. They know how Linney makes my life miserable at school. So why do I have to put up with her during summer vacation too?

S & B won't let her get away w/anything today. Hold on, S is texting me. Lauren's right. Even if they agreed to this, there's no way they'd let That Monster do anything horrible during the party.

If they see it coming, that is.

I just know she's up to something. I tried to tell Becca and Sadie that, but they brushed it off. They're so excited about booking this party that they've looked right past Linney's awfulness. It's like they've forgotten all about what she did with that cake at Molly Campbell's party. She tried to sabotage us there, so what's to keep her from trying again? Why else would she ask *us* to plan the party? It's not like any of us are BFFs with her.

I move the dryer closer to the neckline of the yellow dress and type out a response to Lauren. Wld b better if u were here 2. More of us is safer.

Why are you all ganging up on me? Oh, right. Sadie's probably bugging her to come over too. Not to mention Becca's hourly texts.

Sry. We all want u here.

But I can't. SATs, 'member? I can almost hear Lauren sighing all the way from her house. I still don't get why she feels like she has to study for a test we won't need to take for five or six years.

Will make u those baked pita chips u luv so much. Pllllzzzz????

Nothing. I set my phone down and check the dress. It's dry in spots, but still mostly damp. I'm kind of running out of time, so I switch to drying the construction-zone-orange dress.

I rly can't. Sorry. :(

Great.

"*What* are you doing in my bathroom?" Linney's standing in the doorway, hands on her hips. "You're supposed to be outside, helping set up."

I'm so caught off guard, I whirl around with the hair dryer, blasting hot air right in Linney's face.

"Turn it off!" she squeals, hands in front of her face as her highlighted hair flies up all over the place.

I switch off the dryer and gather up the two dresses

and my phone with my free hand. No way am I sticking around here any longer than I have to. "Excuse me," I say as I take a step forward. "I have to finish setting up."

"Where are you going with my hair dryer, Violet?" She holds out one hand while furiously smoothing her hair with the other. And she gives me this look like she's sure I'm trying to steal her stupid pink dryer.

I hand it back to her but my finger ever-so-accidentally hits the on switch. Hot air blasts out again, messing up all her smoothing work. "Oops," I say as I slide out the door and down the stairs.

"Are they dry?" Sadie grabs the dresses from me the second I walk out the back door.

"Kinda."

"They're still damp! And they'll never dry out here, it's so humid." Sadie's voice is getting that high-pitched, almost-freaking-out tone again. She stops and takes a deep breath. "Okay, it's just a minor setback. That's all. We'll put these two at the bottom of the stack, so maybe we won't even need them. Next time, we'll order at least ten extra dresses." She's making notes in her head, I can tell, even as she bats mosquitoes away from her face. "Lauren's not coming, so we're on our own. You're in charge of the beads and feathers and stuff."

"Really?" I ask, but Sadie doesn't answer. She's standing on her tiptoes, trying to see over the gate and down the driveway to the street.

She's looking for her mom.

I push aside my feelings about That Monster and The Traitor (and the fact that I'm really super annoyed that Lauren isn't coming) and reach out to squeeze Sadie's hand. "Don't worry. She'll be here. There's no way she'd miss two parties in a row."

Sadie gives me a nervous smile.

I take up my station behind a big table covered in baskets of feathers, beads, sequins, sparkly rhinestones, pieces of cloth, and just about anything else you could think of to put on a dress. If I was going to wear that blue dress, I'd want it to be really simple. No extra frou-frou things. The color is perfect just the way it is.

Not that I'd wear a dress, though. So Not Vi.

I swirl around a dish of beads with my finger as I check out the party. Only a few hours here, and then I can ride by Beach Sports on the way home. Buying those green kayaks later this summer will make this party—and Linney—worth it.

Almost all the party guests arrived while I was blow-drying dresses. It's mostly girls from school, but there are a few guys here and there. I guess Linney wants them to be the judges or something. Maybe I should give them a heads-up that they'd better vote for her dress or suffer the consequences. Then again, two of them play on the other beach volleyball team, and I could use them off their game at our next match. I wave at Lance, who grins and rolls his eyes. Bet his mom made him come.

Becca's got poor Ryan cornered over by the gate to the dock. He's twisting one of the tails of his tux jacket. Every time he takes a step sideways, Becca does the same. It's like this hilarious little dance, except she's the only one who's into it. Finally Sadie arrives to save Ryan. She points Becca toward the accessories table, which is covered in shoes, purses, jackets, tights, and feather boas. I don't know who'd want to put on a feather boa in this heat, not to mention tights or a jacket. If you ask me, I'd forget all this stuff—pretty blue dress or not—and just stick with a comfy pair of shorts and a tank top. Oh, wait. I did.

Becca's trying on a pink feather boa when Linney peers around the runway and starts snapping her fingers to get Ryan's attention.

"A-hem!" she says, in a not-at-all-quiet voice.

He leaps up onto the runway, holding a microphone.

A microphone? Seriously, where does Sades find this stuff?

"Ladies and gentlemen! Welcome to the fashion event of the summer: Linney's Sweet Thirteen! May I present your hostess and worldwide supermodel, Linney Marks!"

Three guesses who wrote his script. Hint: not any of us.

Everyone (except me and Sadie) breaks into applause. I give Becca the evil eye and she immediately stops clapping and starts rearranging purses. The feather boa around her neck drags across the table.

Linney sweeps up onto the runway and does this series of model poses. It's so over-the-top and obnoxious, I can't believe I'm the only one having to stuff my fist into my mouth to keep from laughing. Okay, maybe the guys aren't buying it either. Lance has this confused look on his face, and I swear even Ryan cracks a quick smile.

"And now, if the ladies will direct their attention to the tables in back, we have a selection of lovely dresses for you to create your fashion masterpiece, which you'll model for our judges"—Ryan gestures at the boys, who are all clustered together by the snack table—"on this here very stage, in a fierce competition to determine the winner of Linney's Runway." He cocks an eyebrow at the crowd. "You have one hour. Make it work!"

Every girl in the yard flies to the dresses. It's like an exploding rainbow at the table next to me as they fling dresses all over the place.

"Ex-cuse me." Linney pushes through her crowd of guests. "Birthday girl gets to choose first." She snatches the orange dress from the very bottom of the pile. "Perfect," she says, with a quick glance at me.

She is so up to something. She *knows* that one is still damp. But I don't have time to think about it, because approximately twenty girls have descended upon the feathers and sequins and stuff on the table I'm manning.

"Do you have any more green feathers?" Anna Wright asks.

"Where are the pinking shears? Please tell me you have pinking shears!" McKenna Dubray waves around a pair of plain old scissors.

"There aren't enough clear beads!" Ella Hernan shoves the basket under my nose. "I need more clear beads!"

I'm under the table, sweat dripping into my eyes, finding more beads, extra buttons, bottles of glue, peacock feathers—and what in the world are pinking shears anyway?—so I don't even notice the creaking until it's too late.

"Avalanche!" someone yells.

At that second the table bops me on the head. Clutching beads in one hand and lengths of sequins in the other, I can't do anything except watch the legs on one end of the table collapse.

Screams and squeals sound from above. Baskets and beads and scissors rain down from the table into the yard. I can't move. I'm stuck with the table resting on my head and handfuls of . . . stuff.

"Vi? Vi!" Becca's voice is somewhere up there. "Hey, y'all! Boys with the muscles! Help us get this table up."

The weight on my head lifts, and then both Becca and Sadie's faces appear underneath.

"Omigosh, Vi, are you okay?" Becca's putting the back of her hand against my forehead, like I have a fever or something.

Sadie's dumping the beads and sequins from my hands into a basket, and then she and Becca pull me out from under the table.

"What hurts? Do you have a concussion? Blurry vision? How many fingers am I holding up?" Becca shoves two fingers, peace sign–style, right in front of my face.

"I'm fine, really." I push her hand away. And that's when I notice the mess.

Everything—and I mean *everything*—that was on the table is now in the sandy grass in Linney's backyard. Itty-bitty beads and teeny-tiny rhinestones sparkle all over the ground. "Oh, no." I put a hand over my mouth as if that'll make the mess go away.

"It's ruined! You've messed up my whole party, you—you—" Linney appears out of nowhere, sputtering, with the partially sequined orange dress draped over her shoulder.

Sadie's blinking really fast. She's either trying not to cry or one of those beads got in her eye. Finally she puts her hands on her hips.

"Nothing's ruined," she says in a voice that sounds just like her mother's. "Everyone go on to the accessories table, where Becca will help you get whatever else you need. By the time you're done there, we'll have this cleaned up and ready to go."

"Ooh, feather boas!" one of the girls says, and just like that, they're crowding around Becca and the accessories table.

Linney narrows her eyes at us before joining her guests.

"Okay, got that taken care of. Now how in the world are we going to deal with a bedazzled lawn?" Sadie's biting her lip as she studies the ground.

"A vacuum! We could vacuum it up," I say, all triumphantly, as I rub the top of my head where the table whacked it.

"I think we'd get more sand than beads and stuff."

We're quiet for a moment as the shouts and laughter go on at Becca's table. "Try this one! Pink and brown are *perfect* together," Becca's saying to someone.

"If Lauren was here, she'd probably have some amazing idea about how to clean this all up. With magnets or something we'd never think of," Sadie says.

I twist the ends of my ponytail. I really wish Lauren was here too. "I don't think magnets will work."

Sadie gives me this look, like *Obviously, Vi.* "The wet dresses were bad, but this is awful," Sadie finally says. "I don't know how to fix this. We're going to have to refund Linney's mom all the money."

"No way," I say, and I'm surprised at how forceful my voice is. "Nuh-uh. Lauren or no Lauren, we'll figure this out, and we're not giving back a cent. You're Sadie

Pleffer, organizer extraordinaire. You do *not* give up this easily!"

"But . . ."

"What is it your mom always says?"

Sadie wrinkles her eyebrows. "Go big or go home?"

"Not that one. The other one. Something about funeral homes or inheritances or . . . wills, I think."

"Where there's a will, there's a way?" Sadie says.

"That's it! Doesn't that mean if you really, really want something to happen, you have to make it happen?" I kind of feel like I'm coaching a one-girl volleyball team. "And what if your mom showed up right this very second? Wouldn't you want her to see you taking charge and *owning* this party? Not moaning over a bunch of spilled beads." We both turn toward the gate, but, of course, no one's there.

Sadie stops chewing on her lip. "You're right. But how . . ." Her eyes land on the single basket sitting on the table—the one with the beads and sequins I had in my hands when the table fell. "Wait! We have lots of extra supplies under the table. We'll set those out for now, and while they're working with that, we'll pick up as much of the stuff on the ground as we can."

Sadie tightens her ponytail and we swing into

action. Just as we finish putting out all the non-sandy feathers and doodads, the girls start trickling back from Becca's accessories table. While I try to keep Table Avalanche Part Two from happening, Sadie plucks sequins and beads and bottles of glue from the ground.

"Five minutes, fashionistas," Ryan says into the microphone.

"Thank God," Lance says really loudly from across the yard. I peek past the bent heads of the girls at my table to where the guys have pretty much demolished all the food we'd set out earlier. Some of them are huddled around another's phone, probably playing a game. The rest are just sitting in chairs, looking boreder than bored. I think one of them's even fallen asleep.

The girls cut and glue and sew like crazy. Linney pushes aside baskets full of decorations and grains of sand and the occasional pine needle to lay out her dress on the table.

"Perfect, don't you think, Violet?" She twists her lips up into an approving smirk. "I think the Spanish moss really adds something, don't you?"

Why in the world she picked the damp dress, I have no idea. But the thing is hideous (one benefit of hanging out with Lauren is picking up words like "hideous," which is the perfect way to describe Linney's creation). She's cut the hem in a ragged zigzag pattern, so that it kind of looks like the bottom of the witch's costume I wore for Halloween a few years ago. Then she glued long strips of white cloth around the entire dress, so it definitely looks like a traffic cone now. The remaining orange parts are blinged out with so many sequins I can barely stand to look at it.

And the crowning effect? Spanish moss that she plucked from the live oak near the dock and glued to the short sleeves and neckline of the dress. It's possibly the ugliest thing I've ever seen.

"So, do you like?" Linney's looking right at me.

"Um . . . sure." Sadie's standing nearby, and no way am I going to insult Linney in front of her. She's already had enough happen during this party.

Linney's lips turn up into an ugly smile as she eyes me. "Good, because I made it for you. To model on the runway."

Did I mention I was going to murder Becca?

Sadie

TODAY'S TO-DO LIST:
- [ ] return runway to Chamber of Commerce
- [ ] drop microphone back at Darling's DJs
- [ ] arrange for Linney to meet with a horrible accident

Vi's face is turning as orange as the dress on the table next to her, and it's only a matter of time before this gets really ugly (uglier even than that dress, if possible), so I guess it's up to me to save the day.

Again.

I know I'm the one who wanted this business, plus I'm the president so the ultimate responsibility is mine, and I really *am* having fun with it (most of the time), but this party is threatening to be the death of me. For one thing, it seems like everything that could go wrong *is* going wrong. Mom has a name for these events. She calls them "Throw Up Your Hands." Like, at a certain point that's all there is left to do.

Of course, it's just an expression, because Mom would never, EVER give up on a wedding, and I've seen her practically kill herself to make a bad day turn around for a bride. (Funny how she doesn't have the same sense of dedication toward her daughter, since wherever she is right now, it's not here.)

During one of the last "Throw Up Your Hands" we did together, Mom and I had to politely convince the bride's second cousin that she couldn't bring her husband as her guest. Why was it a problem? Oh, only because he was in an urn in her arms. Or at least his ashes were.

I know if I want to make this company work, I have to be just as dedicated. But there are regular problems . . . and then there's Linney. And whatever she's scheming with this whole Vi-has-to-wear-the-dress thing is totally beyond me. I could really use some of Lauren's logical thinking right now, but she's got better things to do, I guess.

I put a hand on Vi's arm and smile at Linney. "What's this all about now?" I ask as sweetly as I can manage.

"I'm simply making a birthday-girl request."

"She made it hideous on purpose," Vi sputters. "It looks like one of those traffic cones. And now she's acting like it's not some kind of jab at my dad. I'm NOT wearing it."

"I don't get it," I say to Linney.

"Well, I'm not feeling good," Linney says with a shrug. "It's messing with my balance, so I don't want to take any chances up there on the runway. The last thing I need on my Sweet Thirteen is a broken ankle, right?"

I squeeze Vi's arm to keep her quiet. I'm pretty sure if I let go, Vi would try to break that ankle herself. After all, Linney had no problem hopping up on the runway and posing away at the start of the party.

"Linney, if you really don't want to model the dress, I'll do it." It's just about the last thing I want to do, especially since that orange looks like one of Lauren's highlighters threw up, but my job—my only job—is to keep the guest happy at all costs.

Linney looks me up and down. "You're not the right size for this dress."

I flick my ponytail over my shoulder, annoyed. "Fine. Becca, can you come over here?"

Linney doesn't blink. "Becca's too petite. This dress

needs someone tall and athletic to make it work. After all, I *do* want to win."

Vi's twisting her hair so hard, it's going to curl up into a bun. She opens her mouth, and I squeeze her arm again.

There is zero chance Linney thinks she's going to win with the monstrosity that is lying on the table oozing moss, and every one of us knows it. Becca jogs over and I watch her try hard not to make a face when she looks at the blob of orange in front of us.

"What's going on?" she asks.

"Linney is feeling . . . unbalanced. She'd like Vi to take her place on the runway. In the dress she designed." It's super hard to keep my voice neutral.

Becca looks at the table, then at Linney, then at Vi, her eyes growing wider. But she takes a cue from me and answers, all nonchalant-like, "Oh. Well, the thing is, Vi was just telling me a few secs ago that she was feeling really icky in the heat today, so it would totally not be the best idea for her to—"

"Ooooh, Lin-bin, let's see what yours looks like!" Mrs. Marks picks exactly that minute to step up to our little group. I mean, props to her for being somewhere her daughter wants her to be, unlike *some* of our moms, but really, could she have worse timing? I suddenly glimpse exactly how this scene is going to play out and I have to swallow down an acid taste in my mouth.

Sure enough, Linney turns her poor-me-I-can't-walk-the-runway act on her mom, and I mean, really, what can we do but nod along when Linney fills her mom in (with big, innocent blinks of her eyes) on her plan to have Vi sub for her so the dress can still compete? The more Linney talks, the redder Vi gets. The whole thing is obviously ridiculous, since Linney has come up with all the rules for this competition anyway and there's no reason she can't enter her dress without a model. It's just a silly party game.

Buuuuuut Mrs. Marks is the one who's paying us. And hopefully referring us to all her friends. So what choice do we have?

I can hardly look at Vi, who I just know is steaming mad. At least I hope she's mad. Mad is way better than sad, which is the other very real possibility.

"I'm not . . ." Vi trails off.

Becca smooths Vi's hair down and says softly, "Why don't I take you inside to change. Maybe you'll let me do something with your hair? And, like, some makeup, possibly? Y'know, just to get in the spirit. Trust me, you're going to rock this ugly dress."

As bad as I feel for Vi, I have to stifle a tiny smile. Becca has been trying to get her mascara wand near Vi's lashes since forever. Or at least since our parents agreed we could wear a little, tiny bit of makeup this year. Becca, of course, owns way more mascara and blush and eyeliner than her mom and dad would ever let her walk out the door wearing.

Becca leads a stunned-looking Vi inside, and I barely have time to watch them disappear before I have to spring back into party-planner mode. I rush over to the waiting girls and tell them about the delay, then ask them to fill out note cards Ryan can use to describe their designs as they come down the runway. After that I have to check the sound system. And make sure Mrs. Marks doesn't examine her grass too closely. And check on the punch we put out to see if it needs more ice. And put out more food, since the guys ate every single crumb on the table. And find seats for the boys who are acting as judges. Oh, and make sure they have scorecards and pens.

Right in the midst of all the chaos, my little sister shows up at the back gate, pacing back and forth like she can't decide whether to come in or not.

I race over. "Iz, what are you doing here? You know this is a private event!"

Izzy pulls a flower off the bush at the garden gate and fiddles with it. "I know. But Mom sent me over to tell you she can't make it. She got stuck on the mainland when they raised the drawbridge."

I groan. On a summer weekend, who knows how many boats will be lined up to pass under the bridge? She could be trapped on the other side for an hour. I instantly go from frazzled to full-out cranky.

"Fine. You told me. Now go," I snap.

Izzy's eyes get all big and I instantly feel terrible for the way I talked to her. I totally get what people mean when they say "Don't shoot the messenger" now. But Mom's not here to yell at, and this party is a disaster, and . . . did I mention Mom's not here?

"Um, so I guess you don't need any extra help? I dressed nice just in case," Izzy says. She backs up so I can see her skirt and shiny shoes.

I sigh and try to be nicer when I say, "Thanks, Iz,

but this is work. We can't have a little kid around—it wouldn't look professional. Plus Linney's got it in for us already, so . . ."

Izzy just nods and backs away from the gate, picking her bike up off the ground and throwing a leg over. She shakes her head a little and pastes a smile on. "Yeah, I get it. Have fun, good luck, break a leg, all that. Guess I'll see you at home."

I watch her pedal away for a second before a squeak from behind me jolts my attention back to the party. Katie Asselin's high heel is stuck in the wet sand. Great. Just great.

I'm on my knees trying to force it out when the party goes completely quiet. It's like that scene from the movies when the music screeches off and everyone turns to stare at something. Except this time it's only a coincidence that one song just ended and the next one hasn't started yet. The everyone-turning-to-stare part, though? That totally happens.

Vi is standing in the doorway to the Markses' house, looking around like she's Dorothy waking up in Oz. She peers around in confusion.

Um, whoa!

I mean, obviously I know Vi is a girl. It's just that she's

really never been all that interested in highlighting that fact. Not because she doesn't care, I don't think, but more because she doesn't have room in her schedule for things she considers unimportant (like mani-pedis, for instance). But Becca is a GENIUS. They were only gone for, like, twenty minutes and somehow it's a whole new Vi.

Vi's *always* been really pretty, except it's not the first thing you notice about her because she doesn't want it to be. But want it or not, it's the first thing everyone's noticing right now. Including the boys. *Especially* the boys. I'm pretty sure a dozen no-see-ums have flown into Lance's mouth in the time he's stood there with it hanging open.

Vi's hair is blown straight and worn down, instead of in its usual ponytail. Becca has clearly talked her into lip gloss and she's in a DRESS. I just need to repeat that. Vi. Is in a dress. And not one of the ginormous Southern belle poufy things from the plantation party that covered every inch of skin, either. I'm guessing no one even notices it isn't exactly the most stylish of dresses, because all they can notice is that Vi's the one wearing it. Truthfully, the orange isn't even such a bad color against her deep tan.

Lauren is gonna be so super bummed she missed

this. Oh well. Every girl here has a cell phone. This will be all over our class by later today.

Vi turns behind her, where a beaming Becca offers her arm to our very wobbly high-heeled friend. For someone who is the queen of balance on a surfboard, it sure doesn't take more than a few inches of stiletto to throw Vi off her game.

She lets a lock of hair fall forward to cover her face as she walks and kind of hides behind it, which is equally weird to see. Usually Vi's completely comfortable in her body. She never seems self-conscious in front of the guys when she's on the beach volleyball court or in her wetsuit in the surf, but she doesn't even lift her head as she walks to line up behind the other girls waiting for the show to start. Instead, she starts picking at her nails.

Wow, I mouth to Becca, who is definitely holding *her* head high.

I know, she mouths back, grinning.

Vi might not be comfortable, but she's totally gorgeous. And—oh boy—*someone* is not happy with all the whispering being about somebody other than the birthday princess herself.

Linney is standing off to the side of the party with her arms crossed.

That probably means I should be doing something to fix the situation, but, hey, she can't complain. Technically, Vi's in a dress walking the runway because Linney insisted. So really, she got exactly what she asked for. Karma, baby.

I know it's a little mean of me, but seeing Linney miserable makes me not-so-cranky anymore. And I didn't even have to knock a bottle of paint on her to get that reaction this time. Although I'm betting Vi was probably expecting me to stand up for her again like that. But this time it's our business on the line. And besides, look at how well it's working out.

I flag down Ryan and move my hand in a circle like I'm winding something up. Hopefully he'll catch on that this is my signal for *Let's get this thing moving.*

He does. Hopping onstage, he grabs the mic and says, "Okay, it looks like the show can go on! Judges, do you have your scorecards? Girls, we ready?"

He gets nods and cheers from everyone, so I rush over to the sound system and switch my playlist to the show music. I picked some really upbeat songs perfect for strutting.

Ryan is an awesome emcee. He reads the note cards describing each dress like he's narrating a commercial.

And his accent makes words like "glamorous" sound super adorable. I totally get why Becca has such a crush.

Because she got in line last, Vi is the final girl to walk the runway. She also doesn't have a note card because I totally didn't think to write her one while everyone else was filling out theirs. Event-planning fail. Luckily, Ryan's acting training must have covered improv, because he totally rolls with it.

"And last up, we have the lovely Vi looking, well, extra lovely." He smiles at her and Vi grimaces, but at least she starts slowly up the runway. A few of the girls who already walked do catcalls. I steal a glimpse at Linney and she is practically purple.

Vi isn't exactly working it like some of the others did—no hip shimmies and pauses midway for twirls for her—but at least she makes it to the end of the runway without tripping in her heels.

"Vi is modeling a creation by designer extraordinaire Linney Marks," Ryan says. I steal a glimpse at Linney, but even the compliment doesn't wipe the scowl off her face. It's all puckered up like she's chewing on a Sour Patch Kid. "I'd call it a masterpiece in texture, and just look at the way the drab green of Spanish moss contrasts with the, uh, vividness of the orange. Linney has gone for an unconventional hemline and really embraced the risk-taking the design world celebrates."

I have to give him credit, I would NOT have been able to come up with anything half as nice to say about a weed-covered Day-Glo dress. Also, I'm thinking the kid really researched his part. He must have binge-watched *Project Runway* all week.

Vi turns, sends a quick glare to Linney, and makes her way back up the runway. Her shoulders sag in relief the second she reaches the picnic blanket we hung to act as a curtain, and she slips behind it.

Ryan is still going. "Okay, we're going to break for a bit of candle-blowing, wish-making, and cupcake-eating, while our esteemed judges tabulate their scores."

Linney manages to recover a little bit once the spot-light turns back to her, but when everyone gathers again on the runway for the judges' pronouncement, she looks ready to spit bullets as Lance breathlessly (and kind of shyly) places a crown on Vi's head and proclaims her the winner. It gets even worse when all the other girls crowd around, telling Vi how awesome her makeover is. Vi's face is maroon under her tan.

Technically, Linney should be happy because her design won, after all. But you can tell just by looking at her that her big plan was one giant B-A-C-K-F-I-R-E.

Like I said: karma, baby.

Too bad Vi looks just as bewildered as Linney about how this all went down. As soon as her admirers break away, Vi beelines for the Markses' back door, and I have to speed-walk to meet her there.

"Vi, you look incredible," I say.

"This dress smells like pond water and the moss itches worse than mosquito bites and this crown is so not me," she answers, pushing past me to get inside the house.

I look helplessly at Becca, right behind me on the patio, but she just shrugs. "She'll be okay. She might just need a little while to process." She pulls out her phone and starts texting. "I'm sending Lo a picture of Vi. *That'll* make her wish she was here."

I hope. Even though we managed to save this party—barely—an extra person would've been really nice. Plus it's just not the same without Lauren. It's like a cake with a slice missing. RSVP was *supposed* to bring us all closer, not drive a wedge between us. Instead, Lauren isn't part of it at all, I'm more annoyed than ever at my mom, and now Vi is mad at *me*. Remind me which part of this is fun?

Becca tugs on my sleeve. "Hey, check it out!"

She grins and points to Linney, who is making her Sour Patch Kids face again, surrounded by girls holding fistfuls of Spanish moss.

We creep closer, in time to hear Anna Wright ask, "Can you just show me how you did that draping with it? I want to look *exactly* as good as you made Vi look."

Becca and I stuff our hands in our mouths to keep from laughing.

Okay, so maybe there are one or two things about this that are fun.

WOOF! WOOF! JOE'S TURNING THREE!
(That's twenty-one in dog years!)

Bring your own canine pal and join Joe and his owner,

Mr. Charles Vernon, for barks and bites on

Saturday, July 18, at one o'clock

Sandpiper Active Senior Living's Party Room

1101 Rosalinde Street

No gifts, please

Leashes will be provided for doggy strolls outside

Party hosted by Mrs. Geraldine "Bubby" Simmons

RSVP to Sadie Pleffer, (910) 555-0110 or

sadie@rsvpmail.com

10

Lauren

entrepreneur noun \ˌäntrəprəˈno͝or,-ˈnər\
one who manages or organizes a business
Use in a sentence:
RSVP is a great opportunity to become an entrepreneur—for people who don't already have ten other things to do in one day.

Hey, baby / I want to take you on a rocket ship to the sky / So we can have a little talk, eye to eye. . . .

Bubby. She made me change her ringtone to this new Harry Hart song because she thinks he's "all that and a bag of chips." Never mind that having a talk eye to eye doesn't make any sense at all.

The song plays again. It's eight p.m., and I've spent all day dodging calls and texts from my friends, bugging me to join them at Linney's. Then Becca sent me this picture of Vi looking like . . . well, not Vi, and I haven't heard anything else. I guess they gave up.

I kind of wish I knew how the party turned out.

Harry Hart starts singing again. To make him shut up, I answer the phone.

Bubby doesn't even say hi. She just jumps right in. "Lo baby, you need to loosen up. I read on the Tweeter that some kids are having a par-tay tonight at the cove. I RSVP'd you. Do you think they'd care if I showed up too? I'd wear my clubbing clothes. And I could oil up ol' Wanda and ride there in style."

I cringe just a little. Wanda is Bubby's fancy new electric old-people scooter, and is short for "wanda around." As in, wander around the mall. Or middle-school parties. The funniest thing about Wanda is that Bubby doesn't even need it. She lives at Sandpiper Beach *Active* Senior Living for a reason. She just likes a "fine set of wheels," she told me when she bought it.

"Bubby, I can't go to a party tonight. I have SAT class in the morning. And it's Twitter, by the way, not Tweeter."

"I know we talked at Bunco today about all of your *responsibilities*." Bubby says "responsibilities" like it's some kind of bad word. "But instead of hanging with a bunch of oldsters like my friends, you should totes be throwing these parties with your girls. Did I tell you that my BFF died last week?"

"What? Bubby, why didn't you say anything?" I picture Bubby alone in her apartment, crying about her friend. I can barely stand my friends planning parties without me, never mind not being here at all. I feel awful for her.

"It's okay, Lo. We were friends in school, but then she moved to Wisconsin and I didn't talk to her again until I found her on the Tweeter last month. Then she died."

"So you're telling me I need to join RSVP before my friends move away and die?"

"Looky here. Before long, you and the girls will be too busy going to work and having your own kids. And then you'll think back to how it was when you were twelve. All of these parties, and the beach, and the cute boys! You'll remember all this great stuff and it'll give you all the feels. But only if you get in on the action! Who knows, you might even go to Atlantic City and flirt with some nice boys on leave and stay up till dawn talking about how amazeballs the future'll be."

Okay, I know she's not talking about me with that

last part. Bubby's actually quiet for a moment and I'm pretty sure I hear her sniffling through the phone. Maybe that friend meant more to her than she let on.

"Bubby?" I say quietly. "Are you all right?"

She clears her throat. "Couldn't be better. Now promise me you'll join your girls and live it up?"

"I'll think about it. I promise." And that's all I can do.

I thought about what Bubby said until I fell asleep last night. It was the first thing that popped into my head this morning even though I had to do a practice math test at SAT class. And I'm still thinking about it as I comb the beach for shells with Vi. To be honest, I really, really want to be part of RSVP. I always have, but I still can't figure out how to make it fit in with everything else I have to do this summer.

"Got it!" Vi sprints through the surf, holding up her prize. Or my prize, really, since she hands it to me. A gorgeous, perfectly formed tiny conch shell.

"How did you spot this?" I ask as I examine the beautiful spiraled shell. Whole conch shells are super rare here, since the ocean gets really rough and tends to break them before they reach shore. I've only ever found a few, and all of those near where Sadie lives, in a protected little cove at the south end of the island.

But never here, in one of the busiest parts of the beach, pretty much right in front of Vi's grandmother's house.

Vi shrugs, like it's no big deal that she found this amazing, rare shell. "It rolled across my foot."

I peer at the sand, looking for more shells. The tide's going out, which is the best time for shell-collecting. It's nice having Vi scoping the sand right next to me. I feel like I've barely seen my friends this week. They were so busy with Linney's party, and I . . . wasn't. Busy with the party, that is. I don't dare tell Vi I'm trying to figure out if I can join or not. She'll tell Sadie and Becca, and then they'll never let up on me till I give in.

"So?" Vi says.

"Soooo . . . ?" I'd love to find another conch, but I suppose I should count myself lucky to have gotten one today. Not that luck has anything to do with it. Luck is something that people make up to explain coincidences. And the probability that another coincidence involving me and a conch shell will happen is pretty low.

"Lauren! Did you hear anything I said?"

I look up. Vi's standing in front of me, hands on her hips.

Then I feel like a huge jerk, because Vi had an awful time at Linney's party yesterday. That's probably what she was talking about. I think. "But it sounds like you had the last say at the end," I tell her.

She rolls her eyes. "I guess. I mean, it was nice seeing Linney all ticked off, but the way Lance and the other guys kept acting was just plain weird. Though Becca was kind of amazing—"

I almost drop my conch shell. "Wait. Did you just say you *liked* Becca's makeover?"

Her face goes red. "Maybe. Just a little. But it's not like I have time to do that stuff every time I go out the way she does. And I'd look pretty silly showing up to swim or play volleyball with a head full of curls and glimmery lip gloss." Then she shakes her head. "You're totally distracting me. That's not what we were talking about."

Shoot. I know what Vi's going to say next. I look past her at the tall redbrick lighthouse that's been on Sandpiper Beach since June 30, 1857. People used to live in the little house attached to it, to take care of the lighthouse and keep the light going, but now it's all automated and no one lives there. Sometimes I think it would be fun to move into the cute matching redbrick house, but then again, the place is probably full of ghosts and I know—

"Laur-*EN*. You're not paying attention at all. Quit stalling and answer, already." Vi's twisting that ponytail again and squinting at me in the bright sun.

"I don't know," I say. And that's the truth. When I came over earlier, Vi laid yesterday's whole awful party down on me. How Linney wanted her to model the dress, and how neither Sadie nor Becca listened to her when she said she didn't want to. And—worst of all—how she thinks it wouldn't have happened the way it did if I'd been there.

Then I got *another* of Becca's texts. This one said, U know u want 2 be / Part of RSVP / Laugh with yr friends / Have fun once again. She's been on a rhyming streak all day. And, if that wasn't enough, Sadie called to ask my opinion on whether going to Party Me Hearties on the mainland is more cost-effective than using the little stationery store on the island.

It's like they know I'm super confused and maybe even *thisclose* to joining. I wonder if Bubby ratted me out.

"'I don't know' isn't an answer," Vi says.

I turn the conch shell over and over in my hand. "But I don't. I think you're right. Becca's too into Ryan to notice anything else, and Sadie's too preoccupied with making the business work. But if I'd been there, we could've figured out what Linney was up to before she even asked you to model that dress."

"It was two against one." Vi kicks a pile of seaweed with her bare toes, which completely freaks out one of the adorable little sandpipers in front of us. The tiny bird goes running so fast, his legs look like the Road Runner's from the Bugs Bunny cartoons. "With you there, I'd at least have had a fighting chance. So now you're going to join, right? Sadie and Becca really want you, too." She looks at me with this hopeful gleam in her eyes.

"I don't know . . . Honestly, I want to. I think it would be fun, and I'm all about helping you and the other girls, but, Vi . . . I just have so much else going on!" Not to mention it's already the second week of July and I've barely touched my summer reading list.

"You wouldn't even have to be the treasurer or anything! I'll keep doing that. All you have to do is show up at the parties," Vi says. She folds her hands like she's praying. "Please? Pretty please?"

"That's not really fair, though. If I joined, I'd feel bad if I didn't help with getting decorations or something." I want to say "YES!" so badly, but that wouldn't be right. If I joined, I'd need to haul my own anchor, as Dad likes to say.

"I don't care!" Vi scoops up something from the sand, examines it, and then throws it back down. "I just want you there. We all do. Think of how good running a business will look on your college applications!"

"Okay, okay, just let me think about it." My phone rings, and I stuff the conch into my pocket as I answer it.

"What up, my Lo?"

"Hi, Bubby," I say. She's probably calling to see if I've joined. I need to change the subject, quickly. "Are you doing all right? You know, about your friend?"

"Oh, Alma? She's singin' with the angels, Lo baby. Don't worry about her. So remember that newbie guy I told you about? The one with the pug? The hot one?" Bubby's talking a mile a minute. I stuff a finger into my other ear to drown out the roaring of the waves and the constant wind. "Of course you do. Anywho, next Saturday is his dog's birthday!"

"His dog has a birthday?"

"Everyone has a birthday, silly. But here's my point—I want to throw him, and the dog I guess, a birthday party! And I want you girls to plan it. Isn't that the most awesome news? I bet you're squeeing right now."

Bubby should know I don't squee. I don't think I've ever squeed in my entire life. "But, Bubby, I'm not part of—"

"So you'll do it? Don't forget to find me a dog. I can't host a dog birthday party without a dog. A little poodle would be ubercute. If anyone can find the perfect dog, you can. I knew you'd make the right decision about joining your friends. Thank you, Lo baby! Kisses!" Bubby makes smooching noises through the phone and hangs up.

I end the call and stare at my phone. A wave smacks against my legs, drenching one side of my shorts, but I don't move.

"Lauren? What was that about?" Vi's stopped turning cartwheels in the surf and is waiting for the news.

"I think my grandmother just cajoled me into joining RSVP." (Cajole: convince someone, like your overly busy granddaughter, to do something, like joining her friends' party-planning business.)

Vi scoops up my backpack from the sand and holds it out. Then she laughs.

"What?" I take the backpack and slide my new shell into the zippered pocket.

"Your initials." She points at the white letters stitched onto the front of the bag. LPS. "You do have a P name—Phoebe. See, it was meant to be!"

RSVP. Rebecca, Sadie, Vi, and me—Lauren Phoebe.

You would not believe how hard it is to borrow a dog. Mrs. St. Clair next door looked like I'd asked to take her Chihuahua to Mars instead of Sandpiper Active Senior Living to be fawned over by a bunch of sweet old people. Mrs. O'Malley said her yappy little terrier was "far too delicate" for a party. And apparently Cooper, the black Lab who lives at Polka Dot Books next to Becca's house, is strictly a bookstore-only dog. Vi offered her big orange cat, Buster, but somehow I didn't think Buster would really like going to a party full of dogs.

Finally Becca's dad tracked down a dog whose owner was willing to let him go for the day. Of course, the dog turned out to be a huge, slobbery Saint Bernard named Custard Van Twinkle.

"He's *perfect*!" Bubby exclaims when I arrive with Custard Van Twinkle at Sandpiper Active Senior Living's party room. She bends down to one knee and rubs her hands on either side of Custard's head. "Who's a good doggy? Who's gonna help me nab cute

Mr. Vernon? Who?" she says in a baby voice.

Custard responds by shaking his head and flinging drool across the room.

Bubby stands up and squeezes me into a hug. "I'm so glad you decided to join your friends."

I wrap my arms around her and hug, thinking of Alma and Atlantic City. Bubby smells of baby powder and some kind of flowery perfume, and I don't know what I'd ever do without her.

Something wet thwacks against my leg, and I look down to see Custard drooling on me. "Bubby? Can you hang on to the dog so I can help set up?"

"Oh, I can't, Lo baby. I have to get these curlers out of my hair before Mr. Vernon sees me. And I have to decide what to wear. What do you think, jeggings? Would that look like I'm trying too hard?"

Although anything would be better than the hot-pink robe she has on right now, I cannot handle seeing my grandmother in jeggings. "Um, Becs?" I wave her over from where she's arranging doggy goody bags.

"Hey, Bubby!" She flings her arms around my grandmother in a bone-crushing hug. "Cute earrings! Where did you get those?"

Bubby touches the dangly silver hoop hanging from her right ear. "Oh, these ol' things? Picked them up at the mall on the last trip into Wilmington."

"Becca, Bubby wants to know if she should wear jeggings." I give Becca a please-convince-my-grandmother-this-would-be-a-horrible-idea look.

"I know! Why don't we go pick something out together?" Becca loops her arm through Bubby's and the two of them go chattering off toward Bubby's apartment.

Leaving me with Custard Van Twinkle.

I've never had any pets, so I'm not entirely sure what to do with him. I squat down in front of his droopy face and sad-looking eyes. "Hey, Mr. Van Twinkle. I have to help put out treats for your buddies. Can you take a nap or sit down or something?"

And just like that, Custard Van Twinkle lumbers over to one of the dog beds Sadie thought to get from the pet store, turns around a few times, and then curls up and closes his eyes.

Huh.

So I help Sadie and Vi with the bows-and-bones-themed decorations, make sure there are enough bags and mops in case someone has an "accident," and admire the dog-friendly cake. ("Dog-friendly meaning made for dogs, not people," Sadie says.) As I arrange the chairs into what Sadie calls "conversation clusters," listen to Vi recount the morning's beach volleyball game, and reassure Sadie that this time her mom might actually show up, I realize I'm having fun.

Well, of course I'm having fun. I knew I would. The problem isn't that. It's more like how can I possibly commit to doing this once or twice a week and still have time for everything else? I mean, helping run a business would look amazing on my college applications, that's for sure. The money I earn will go right into my savings account, and that's definitely not a bad thing. I know Vi was thrilled when she suggested having cake for the dogs' owners in addition to the dog-friendly cake and I was there to back her up. And Sadie and Becca were so happy to hear that I wanted to join that the people on the next island over could probably have heard them squealing. So if I'm making a pros-and-cons list in my head, that's five pros and one con. And no question that I should join RSVP.

Ugh. Sometimes I hate being so logical.

Guests and their dogs are starting to arrive, but there's no sign of Bubby and Becca. Finally, I spot Becca's red hair peeking in the door.

"What's going on?" I ask.

"Bubby's waiting for Mr. Vernon to get here. She wants to make an entrance."

Seriously? "Please tell me she's not wearing jeggings."

Becca shakes her head. "No, but she looks so cute that Mr. Vernon will be drooling more than Custard Van Twinkle."

Great. Grandmothers are supposed to bake you cookies and wear aprons and give you a five-dollar bill on your birthday. Or spout folksy little sayings, like Vi's Meemaw. They are not supposed to have crushes on other people's grandfathers and say things like "hottie" and wear cooler clothes than their granddaughters. Not that I'd trade Bubby for anything, but sometimes I wish she was a little more . . . grandmotherly.

"Ooh, there he is!" Becca squeals and points across the room.

A dapper white-haired man in a polo shirt and khaki pants stands near the cake table with a snub-nosed pug in his arms. The door opens wider, and Bubby struts in, aiming straight for Mr. Vernon.

I have to give Becca credit. Not only is Bubby *not* wearing jeggings, but she's actually dressed in a nice long floral skirt, a yellow top, and cute yellow sandals. And a blond wig. I have no idea where that came from, but whatever. "Thank you," I whisper to Becca.

She grins. "She really wanted the jeggings, but I convinced her that Mr. V would be more impressed if she dressed up."

Bubby's already talking before she even reaches Mr. Vernon. She steps over someone's Boston terrier and immediately starts cooing at the pug in Mr. Vernon's arms. Mr. Vernon takes a step back. Bubby steps forward, and now she's got him pinned against the cake table. He looks over her shoulder like he's searching for an escape route.

Someone next to me giggles. Vi.

I look at her and raise my eyebrows.

"If you'd seen the way Becca trapped Ryan at Linney's party, you'd be laughing too," she whispers in my ear.

Becca, however, is frowning. "Why isn't he impressed? He just looks like he wants to run away."

Vi buries her face in her arm and starts coughing, probably to hide her laughter.

"Well . . ." I try to think of the best way to say this. "She's coming on a little too strong, don't you think?"

But before Becca can reply, Sadie claps her hands.

"Attention, everyone. I would just like to thank you all for being here to celebrate Joe's birthday." Sadie gestures at the pug in Mr. Vernon's arms.

Why would anyone name a dog Joe?

"We have a fun afternoon planned for y'all. First up, we thought we'd do a few doggy games," Sadie says.

Next to me, Becca snorts. "I'm still not convinced we're gonna be able to get a slew of dogs to play anything besides Sniff the Butt."

I bump my hip into hers, but also give her a be-quiet look.

Sadie doesn't acknowledge our giggles, just keeps right on talking. "We've got a treasure hunt for a hidden bone, and then we'll have a talent show where your dogs can show off their best tricks. If any of them know the command 'speak,' they can join along in singing 'Happy Birthday' to Joe before they dive into the dog-friendly cake. And we have plenty of food for you owners, too. So, for now we can mingle, and we'll make another announcement in a couple minutes to start the first game. Have fun, everyone!"

Sadie goes back to arranging the plates and silverware we borrowed from the dining room, while Vi leads a guest's dog outside to do doggy business. I grab Becca by the arm and tug her over to help put some space between Bubby and Mr. Vernon, but we're only halfway there when it happens.

Just as Bubby reaches out to pet him again, Joe leaps from Mr. Vernon's arms and sprawls onto the cake table.

"No!" Sadie yells, and snatches the cake away just in time.

The poor dog makes a run down the table as Mr. Vernon finally springs—well, as good as a seventy-five-year-old man can spring—into action. His pug flies off the end of the table onto a stack of extra dog beds, then scrambles up and races across the room on his stubby little legs.

"Joe! Come back!" Mr. Vernon jogs after his dog, with Bubby right behind him.

I'm still wondering why in the world he'd name a dog Joe when Custard Van Twinkle starts barking. The other dogs join in, and before any of us can do anything, Custard is on the chase, right behind Joe, with at least ten more dogs on their heels.

They weave through the legs of the guests, all of whom are calling to their dogs. Then Joe takes a hard right and aims straight toward the back door, which Vi's just opened.

"Vi, the dogs! Close the door!" Sadie screams, still clutching the cake in both hands.

But it's too late. Custard Van Twinkle jumps up with a friendly "woof," placing two front paws on Vi's chest and knocking her right to the ground. She drops the leash she was holding, but she recovers quickly. She snags the leash to the poodle, then rolls to her knees and shoves the door closed. But by that point Custard and Joe are high-tailing it in opposite directions across the long lawn of Sandpiper Active Senior Living.

11

Becca

Daily Love Horoscope for Scorpio:
Venus is aligned with Pluto. Something you thought you needed might already be in your possession.

"I . . . can't . . . run . . . any . . . more," I force out through gasps for air. I prop my hands on my knees and wait for my heart to stop slamming against my rib cage. Ick.

Sadie's almost to the lighthouse, but she stops and puts one fist on her hip. Calling above the wind and the waves crashing, she says, "Don't you quit on me now, Becca Elldridge! We have to find these dogs and get them back safely."

She jogs toward me, also huffing and puffing (but

maybe not as bad as me) and lowers her voice.

"And when we do, we are totally putting an amend-ment in our company bylaws. No events involving ani-mals. EVER. Possible exceptions for marzipan ones on top of cakes. I swear, after the whole thing with Fake Max and the seagull, you would have *thought* I'd learned my lesson."

She reaches me, sticks out her hand, and helps me up.

"Got it. No animals. I vote 'yay,'" I say.

Sadie smiles. "Okay, so we've covered the town square and the gazebo. We let your parents know at the Visitor's Center, Lauren's checking the marina and the souvenir shops, and Vi's looking by the shuffleboard courts. That leaves the lighthouse, right?"

I sigh and start trudging through the sand in the direction of the redbrick building when a movement to my left catches my eye. A furry movement. Kind of like a tail wagging.

"Sades, hold up!" I point to a fleck of brown twitch-ing back and forth in the deep dune grass.

"Uh-oh," Sadie says.

Uh-oh is right. If that's really Custard Von Whatever Whatever, we're in big trouble. Because he's picking his way through the dune grass in a protected area. Like, an area where sea turtles lay their eggs that abso–posi–lutely cannot be disturbed, because then the baby turtles could die and stuff! Plus the town is crazy about keeping the dunes up because they stop the island from eroding into nothingness. And we can't go after him because the fine for walking in there is like a trillion gazillion dollars.

"What are we supposed to do now?" I wail.

Sadie shoots me a don't–be–so–melodramatic look. I am a master at interpreting that look. Let's just say I get it from my friends . . . frequently. And also from some not-friends.

"We'll walk up to the edge and call for him. I bet he comes right out." Sadie is already marching her way to the dune.

"Here, Custard Von Something-Ridiculous!" I call.

Another look from Sadie. "It's Custard Van Twinkle."

"Oh, 'cause that's so much better?"

Sadie smiles and starts clapping her hands. "Here, boy! Here, doggy. I have a treat for you. . . ."

She dangles a dog biscuit in the air in front of her. The tail retreats farther into the grass, and I moan.

"It's not working!"

"I know," Sadie says, and we lock eyes with despair.

An earsplitting whistle cracks the air to our right, and

Sades and I both swing our necks like we're marionettes. A giant drooly Saint Bernard comes crashing out of the dune grasses and sea oats and pulls up at a dead stop in front of a dripping-wet Ryan. Both of them shake water (or drool, in Custard's case) from their hair/fur.

Ryan smiles at us, drops his boogie board into the sand, and reaches down to pet the dog. "Looked like you needed a hand."

"Wow. Your whistle's almost as loud as Vi's. Thank you sooooo much," Sadie says. I'm still working on closing my jaw while Sadie launches into a whole account of what happened at the party and the hunt for the missing dogs.

"We still don't know where Joe is, but I'm hoping someone back in town has found him by now. There's too much sand whipping around today to pull out my cell phone on the beach, but as soon as I can figure out how to get this guy back, I can find a spot to text Vi and get the scoop."

"Here, will this work?" Ryan takes the long black rope attached to his boogie board and slides one end under Custard Von Rip Van Winkle's collar before knotting it. Granted, there's a giant boogie board at the other end of it, but it's totally a leash.

I finally snap out of my trance. "That's, like, totally genius, Ry! You're so smart!"

Ryan smiles a little (sort of) in my direction and hands the boogie board over to Sadie. "One dog. Delivered. I'm all done here, so, if you want, I can walk him back to wherever he needs to be, and you can keep looking for the other escapee."

Omigosh, omigosh. Here's my chance to get Ryan all to myself. FI–NAL–LY.

I tuck my elbow through Sadie's.

"Sades has her bike at the end of the boardwalk, and she could totes ride back with Twinkly here running alongside. Sooo much faster. But if you really do have some time, it would be ah-mazing if you could help me look for Joe. I'm super-duper worried about him."

"Um . . . ," Ryan says, not looking either of us in the eye.

Sadie glances over at me and gives a helpless shrug before saying, "You know what, Ryan? If you wouldn't mind riding my bike back to the Active Senior Living with this guy, that would be really great of you. You can just leave the bike there and I'll grab it later. Becca and I will head into town and text Vi to see if anyone's found Joe."

Um, hello, bestie??? Did you *not* catch on to my

diabolical plan to be alone with Ryan? *What the what?!*

Ryan grins at Sadie and reaches over to grab his boogie board (with giant dog attached) back from her.

"Cool," he says. "I'll stick around the center for a bit. Maybe I'll see you guys back there."

He waves and starts up the boardwalk that crosses over the protected dunes.

"There's cake! Help yourself! Make sure you ask which cake is the people one, though," Sadie yells at his back as he disappears.

As soon as he's out of sight, I punch Sadie on the arm. "What were you thinking?! I could have had hours and hours alone with Ryan!"

Sadie gives me this look like she feels sorry for me, which I so completely do not get. She grabs my hand and we start trailing Ryan up the boardwalk. When we get to the top part of the dune, I spot Ryan, way off in the distance, turning the corner on Sadie's bike.

Le sigh.

Sadie squeezes my hand and says, "Becs, you know I, like, totally love you and whatever. You're one of my very best friends."

"Yeeeeaaah," I answer, drawing out the word like it has a question mark at the end.

"Well, I mean, I just wonder if you might be, um, coming on a little . . ." She pauses and uses her other hand to brush a piece of hair out of her eye.

I wait. A little *what*?

"Um, maybe a little bit strong. With Ryan. I mean, it's not, like, embarrassing or anything, just maybe . . . I don't know. I'm just not sure he's Mr. Right for you, like you think."

I blink at her a few times. What is she even talking about? Omigosh, does *Sadie* like *Ryan*?

"Do you like Ryan?" I blurt out before I can even think about it.

"What? Why would you—BECCA! No!"

She looks so horrified that I have to ask, "But he's cute, right?"

Sadie smiles now. "Totally cute. Adorable accent. Super nice. It's just . . ." Sadie blows her bangs out of her eyes again and sighs. "I'm really, really sorry, sweetie. I just don't know if he's that into you. Which is totally his loss. Completely. Because you're amazing."

We reach the end of the boardwalk and it's like I'm in a weird daze while I brush the sand off my feet and find my sandals. What does she mean, not that into me? Like, he doesn't like me? Like he *never* liked me, even a

little bit, this whole entire time? I was 84 percent positive he liked me at least a little bit. I take a few deep
breaths of the salty sea air and let the scent tickle my
nose while I process this.

Then I moan. It's just what I do.

"But Ryan was my best chance for a boyfriend this
summer!"

Sadie studies me for a second and my pout wilts a
little. It's hard to keep up the drama around Sades 'cause
she's so totally no-nonsense. Which she gets from her
mom. Sadie's eyebrows pucker like she's having some
deep thought and she taps her shoe against her thigh.

"Interesting. Very interesting."

What's so interesting about the fact that I've essen-
tially spent half the summer on a useless mission and
probably humiliated myself a gazillion million times?

"What?" I snap.

Sadie has both her ballet flats on now and my sandal
straps are buckled, so we start walking up the little side
road. I'm dying to hear her answer, but there's something I have to do first. I tug on Sadie's arm and she
smiles and rolls her eyes. She knows I won't pass by the
mermaid without stopping.

We pause in front of the pale yellow house on the

corner and both reach down to scoop a penny from a giant oyster shell full of shiny coins. After a billion zillion trips to the beach, I don't need to read the sign to know what it says, but it's tradition, so I recite it out loud like always.

"Take a penny from the dish,
Close your eyes and make a wish.
Tell it to the mermaid true,
All her luck will come to you."

When I was little I used to make every wish be that we could stop at the Variety Shoppe for an ice-cream cone on the way home, and Dad must have known this, because we almost always did.

Today I close my eyes and whisper under my breath, "I wish I could understand boys."

Let's see the mermaid tackle that one!

I squeeze the penny in my hand (tradition), and toss it into the tiny bright blue pool of water at the painted base of the mermaid statue. Sadie's lands with a plink beside mine.

She links her arm through mine and we start walking again.

"I just have this theory," she says as we cross Coast-line Drive. "Humor me for two seconds and tell me what you like about Ryan."

About Ryan? Where do I begin? "Well, I mean, even you admitted that he's super cute. And you've totally heard his accent, right? I mean, there is nooooo denying the accent."

Sadie just mmm-hmms.

Then she says, "Okay, so, but those are both physical things, and you might act like it for fun sometimes, but I know for a fact you are not a shallow person, Becca Elldridge. So what else? What do you like about him as a person?"

I have to think about this. I have to think *hard* about this. Finally I say, "Oh! His drama stuff. He wants to be an actor."

"Does he?" Sadie asks, and one of her eyebrows pokes up, along with the corners of her lips. She's all smug about some aha moment she's had.

"Um, hello. Are we both sharing this planet? Because if so, you would have totally noticed the kid barely ever changes out of that drama camp T-shirt."

"Oh, I've noticed *that*. But wanting to go to a fun camp and wanting to devote yourself full-time to a profession are two different things. So I was just curious if he wanted to go to acting camp or if he wanted to be an actor."

I'm really not sure I see the difference. He's been so excited to do all the acting gigs we threw at him. Definitely, positively that means he wants to be an actor. Obviously.

"I don't know. I give up. What's the answer?" I ask.

"Oh, *I* don't know. Because *I've* never asked him. And it sounds like you haven't either. Hey, so how come he's spending all summer with his great-aunt, anyway? Where are his parents?"

I think hard again. I know this one. I *know* we talked about this when we first met.

"Yes! I remember! They're on a research trip."

Sadie turns the corner, heading for the gazebo and Merlin in the town square. She looks over her shoulder at me. "That sounds amazing. What are they researching?"

Annnnnnnd, I have no idea. I never asked.

"I don't know," I mumble. "What's the point of this Twenty Questions About Ryan, anyway?"

Sadie slows to let me catch up, then puts her hand on my arm.

"Well, your first reaction was to be upset about not

having a boyfriend, not upset because *Ryan* wasn't acting on any of your I-like-you hints."

I still don't get it.

"I still don't get it," I say.

"I'm just saying, maybe you're more upset about the idea of not having *any* boyfriend, versus not having *Ryan* for a boyfriend."

Oh. *Ooooooooooh*.

I'm quiet while she works her cell phone, even when she lets out a yelp a few seconds later. "They found Joe! He was eating Mrs. O'Malley's hydrangeas!"

I manage a half smile. Sadie plops down on the steps of the gazebo and pats the spot next to her. When I sit, she puts her arm around my shoulder and squeezes tight.

"Becs, can I ask you something?"

I nod. A few kids are playing Frisbee on the grass and there's a lawnmower somewhere nearby, but otherwise, it's pretty quiet. Merlin the Marlin is staring down at us with his shiny brass eyes.

"Why's it so important to have a boyfriend, anyway? I mean, how come you can't just let it happen, like, naturally, or whatever?"

I stare at an ant on the step below me trying to cart

away a crumb on his back. It's like he has the weight of the whole world on him and he's just plugging away at it. I kind of feel like that too sometimes. Maybe it wouldn't be so bad to let Sades in on my secret.

I take a deep breath.

No, I can't.

Yes, I can.

Nope. Can't.

Another deep breath.

Okay, going for it.

"It's for my songs. I need one for my songs, okay?"

Sadie stops tapping her feet. I don't look away from the ant, but I can tell Sadie is staring at me. She probably has a bunch of wrinkles in her forehead.

"Your . . . songs? What songs?"

I pick at a piece of peeling paint on the step and break off a tiny section. I use it to scoop up the ant with his crumb and set him down on the sidewalk another step below. There. Hopefully I helped him out a little.

"In my notebook. That's what I write in there. I know y'all always wondered. But the thing is, I can't possibly ever, ever write a real and genuine song unless I fall in love. And I can't fall in love if I can't get a guy to even want to spend five milliseconds in my presence."

Sadie squeezes my shoulders again. "First of all, plenty of guys would be happy to spend way more than five milliseconds in your presence. But also, you write songs? That's kind of super cool, Becs! Why didn't you tell us?"

"I don't know. I guess it felt too private to share just yet. And seriously, you have to totally, completely pinkie swear you won't tell anyone else. Not even Vi and Lo. I was waiting to surprise you when I had an awesome song all written and worked out on my guitar and everything. Guess *that's* not gonna happen."

Sadie stands up and brushes off her butt. She holds out her hand and pulls me up. "Another 'first of all.' Ready? First of all, I don't know what we're thinking, because we're totally missing out on cake right now. Second of all, Becs? You are so awesome. There's tons of other kinds of stuff to write about. Tons."

"Yeah, but all the radio plays are songs about love. Songs that make people feel things."

Sadie is quiet for a minute. "Well, who says it has to be about boy love? There's a million other kinds of love. Like, what do you love the most?"

This time I don't even have to think hard at all. "All of you. Lo. Vi. Hanging out, us four."

Sadie grins at me. "Well, there you go then."

I'm working up a good argument to this in my head when I realize something. She might be right. Out of the blue, a line comes to me.

> With friends like you to bump
> through life with

It's teasing me and I know there's more there, but before I can concentrate enough to capture it, we're interrupted by what sounds like an ice-cream truck blaring its old-timey music.

We spin around to see Lauren's Bubby tearing up the street in one of those electric scootery things old people ride around the grocery store in, waving her hand all around to get tourists to step aside. And the music? Is totally her horn.

"Wanda and I came to hurry you slowpokes along. We're waiting for you before we bark 'Happy Birthday' to Joe." She taps the side of the scooter, which has WANDA written out in glittery gold script.

Sadie looks at me and I look at her. The second we

catch each other's eyes, we start laughing so hard tears are streaming down our faces. Bubby just sits there on her scooter with her hands on her hips.

"Are you two done laughing at me? I know I'm not looking fantabulous at the moment with this wind whipping my wig all over the place. And Wanda is none too easy to drive like a lady in this skirt. Honestly, Becca, you should have skipped saying 'Yes to the Dress' and signed off on those jeggings. I totes mcgoats would've gotten here faster if I didn't have to keep the whole town from seeing my knickers as I drove. Now bust a move, ladies. Becca, you promised to teach me nail art later."

With that, I have to clutch Sadie to keep from falling over.

Vi

12

S'MORES COOKIE BARS

Ingredients:

¾ cup graham crackers, crumbled

4 tbsp butter, melted

½ cup butter, softened

¾ cup sugar

½ cup brown sugar

1 egg

½ tsp vanilla

1 ¼ cup all-purpose flour

½ tsp baking soda

½ tsp salt

1 cup chocolate chips

½ cup mini marshmallows

1 chocolate bar

Preheat oven to 350°F. Mix graham cracker crumbs with melted butter. Place a sheet of parchment paper into the bottom of a square 8" x 8" baking pan, and then press the graham cracker mixture into the bottom of the pan to make the crust. Cream the softened butter, add in the sugar and brown sugar, and cream until fluffy. Mix in egg and vanilla. Combine the flour, baking soda, and salt. Mix well. Add the flour mixture to the butter-sugar mixture and combine. Fold in chocolate chips and marshmallows. Spoon the mixture on top of the graham cracker crust (try to make it as even as possible, although it won't be perfect). Bake for 20 minutes. While the cookie bars are baking, break the chocolate bar into pieces and place it in the freezer. About 8–10 minutes before the cookie bars are finished, you can sprinkle extra marshmallows over the top. Then let the cookie bars finish baking. When done, place pieces of chocolate bar on the top. Let the cookie bars cool completely before cutting.

**Great for when you just want something different from regular s'mores.*

**Perfect for hanging out on the beach when your parents won't let you build a bonfire!*

*T*hat's all the flyers," Sadie says as she appears on the steps in the *Purple People Eater*'s cabin.

"I'll make more. I can't believe we don't have a party booked today. What am I going to do?" Becca wails from where she's lying on the floor near the flashlight bucket. She must be really distracted if she doesn't care how much old yacht dirt is probably attaching itself to her ruffly shirt and pink shorts right this very minute.

"Um, chase that poor guy around some more?" Lauren teases.

Becca makes a face, but doesn't actually say anything about Ryan. Which is So Not Becca.

"Anyway, I know what I'm going to do," Lauren says. "Take a practice SAT and get some summer reading done. Have y'all finished the list yet? I can't believe it's almost the end of July and I've just started. If I don't watch it, I'll start turning into Zach!"

Becca makes a moaning sound, Sadie doesn't even answer—she's looking off into space—and I shake my head. I haven't cracked any of those summer books yet.

"Hey, Sades? You okay?" I reach over and tap her arm. She hasn't moved from the bottom of the steps.

"Yes. No. Not really. Everything seemed to be going great with the business, and now . . . nothing." She sits on the bottom step and rests her chin in her hands.

"We need to do more than flyers." Lauren's folding up a piece of paper into a fan. It's about nine hundred degrees inside the *Purple People Eater* today.

"But what?" I ask.

"Don't look at me," Becca says with her arms over her face. "I'm the worst Queen of Booking and Advertising who ever existed in a hundred million billion years."

"You are not," I tell her. "You've made sure we have plenty of flyers to go around, and you got us those great business cards."

"Whole lot of good any of that's doing," Becca says.

"We need to brainstorm new ideas," Lauren says as she fans her face with the folded paper. "Why don't we all come up with five ideas over the weekend, and we'll pick the best ones to implement."

"To what?" Becca lifts an elbow to eye Lauren.

"Implement. To take action on, or put into practice."

Sadie perks up a little. "That sounds good. We can meet back here on Monday. Everyone come up with good ideas, okay?"

Both Sadie and Lauren are up the stairs before Becca sits up. "Wait, are y'all leaving? But I don't have anything to *do* today."

"You can keep time for my practice test," Lauren calls from the deck above.

"Or go grocery shopping with me," Sadie yells. Sadie's always the one who has to go to the grocery store. Her mom's way too busy with weddings to buy peanut butter or eggs. I mean, I obviously do the shopping for Dad and me too, but the difference is that I enjoy it.

Becca makes a face. "I'd rather hang out at the Visitor's Center. Hey, Vi, maybe we can go to the beach?"

I'm still trying to figure out why Becca's not using her free time to flirt with Ryan. But wait . . . maybe that means . . .

I shove the damp strands of hair that've come loose from my ponytail away from my face. "I kind of have another idea. Can you come over for a little while?"

A huge grin floats across Becca's face. "Yes! We could bake cookies or something."

"Or something." The breeze outside feels so, so, so good after being cooped up in the *Purple People Eater*. As we walk down the dock, lagging behind Sadie and Lauren, I decide I have to tell Becca what it is I really want. "So . . . remember That Mons—I mean, Linney's party?"

"I don't think any of us will ever forget that party." Becca lifts her eyebrows at me.

"Quit looking at me like that!"

"Then why did you bring up the party?"

I roll my bike away from the marina's office. I don't know why I'm so embarrassed to ask Becca. I guess because what I want is just So Not Vi. But if I want something to be more Vi-ish, then it doesn't have to be So Not Vi anymore, right? I can change my mind about what I like and don't like whenever I want. I mean, it's not as if there's a list somewhere saying what I can and can't like.

Then why is this so hard?

"Vi?" Becca's pedaling double-time to keep up with me as I fly down Sandpiper Drive, speeding past the pastel-colored houses that line the street. "Wait, where are we going? Your house is the other way."

I slow down to let Becca catch a breath. "We kind of have to stop at your house first."

"We do? Why?"

"Because there's some stuff we'll need."

"Okaaaay. Plain old chocolate-chip or sugar cookies are fine, you know. They don't have to be anything
fancy," Becca says as we roll up her gravel driveway.

"It's not about cookies."

Becca lifts her eyebrows again.

Just spit it out already, Vi. "You need your makeup
bag and some hair stuff so you can show me what you
did at Linney's party." I say it all so fast that Becca's just
standing there, holding her bike and staring at me.

And not saying anything.

"Ugh, this is so embarrassing. You don't have to do
it. Never mind. Let's just go bake cookies." I'm grabbing
the handlebars of my bike when Becca finally speaks.

Well, she doesn't exactly speak. More like squeals.

I turn around. Her bike's fallen to the ground and
she's jumping up and down and clapping her hands.
"Makeover! Really, Vi, really?! Eek! I'll be right back!"

Then she's racing up the wooden stairs to her front
door, leaving me in the driveway. Becca's house is right
next door to Polka Dot Books and across the street
from the Pipin' Hot Café. The café is cooking something with basil, and it's making my stomach rumble.
Hmmm . . . I put a pizza together last night. I think I'll

pop it in the oven when we get back to my house.

Becca's gone so long that I start counting the ants crawling along one of the wooden pilings holding up Becca's house. Almost all the houses on the island, except the older ones like Lauren's, are raised off the ground. They're held up with thick wood posts called pilings. That way, if a hurricane hits and there's flooding, the houses will stay dry inside.

The one thing that really freaked me out when Dad and I moved into Meemaw's house on the beach was how, at night in bed, I could feel the entire house sway just a teeny-tiny bit whenever the wind gusted. The trailer park's on the other side of the bridge, not even on the island, so the whole shaky-house thing was new for me. I'd probably felt it sleeping over at Becca's or Sadie's before, but I'd never really noticed it. Not until I had to sleep through it almost every single night.

"Ready?" Becca calls from the top of her stairs. She starts down with a suitcase thumping after her.

"What in the world? How much makeup do you have?" I stare at the navy blue suitcase bumping its way down the steps.

"Oh, Vi. Sweet, sweet, innocent Vi. It's not just

makeup, silly." Becca thumps down the last stair and climbs onto her bike, holding the suitcase handle with one hand. "We ride!" She pedals off, all wobbly with the suitcase rolling alongside her.

What have I gotten myself into?

We bike the block and a half back toward the beach, Becca dragging that suitcase the whole time. We pass Beach Sports, where those gorgeous green kayaks are still sitting outside, just waiting for me to buy them. When we hang a left onto Coastline Drive, Becca's suitcase flips over and drags in the sand that's always on the sides of the road. Becca doesn't pause. She just lifts it up and lets it settle back on its wheels. Like she does this all the time or something.

We roll up to Meemaw's and park our bikes on the shady concrete driveway under the house. No car, so Dad must still be at work. When it's nice out, he works seven days a week. We (and the suitcase) tromp up the stairs, which are painted white to match the trim on the house. The rest is done in this pretty, soft yellow, which always reminds me of lemonade. A little sign on the porch railing lets everyone know that Meemaw named her house Morning Sky. The second we're above the dune line, the wind off the ocean smacks us in the face.

Becca sighs and stares up at the house as I wrestle with the lock on the door.

"I love this place," she says as she wraps her hand around her hair to keep it from flying all over. "You're so lucky to live here."

Which I know. And she knows I know. Meemaw's house is huge. Not just huge compared to the trailer Dad and I used to live in, but HUGE compared to most of the other houses lining the beach. It has this amazing wraparound porch on both floors. I even have a door in my room that opens right onto the second-floor porch. From there, I can see all the way down to the pier, and sometimes I swear that if I look hard enough, I can spot Europe. Or Africa. Whatever's straight across the ocean, anyway.

"This morning I saw dolphins before I left for volleyball," I tell Becca as the door finally swings open. Buster appears out of nowhere and winds himself around my ankles.

"Ah-mazing." She hauls the suitcase in, tracking sand across Meemaw's white tile. Luckily, Meemaw's nowhere close enough to see, and Dad and I really don't care about a little sand. This is the beach, after all.

"Ta-da! Prepare to be dazzled!" Becca's already

pulling the suitcase up the stairs. Buster's jumping from step to step, swatting at the luggage tag hanging from one of the zippers.

My stomach rumbles again. "Let me preheat the oven for this pizza first."

"Okey-dokey. Meetcha upstairs," Becca calls from the top of the landing.

I run into the kitchen (the seriously massive, incredible kitchen), and flip the oven temperature to 425 degrees. Then I pull out the homemade pizza I made last night and set it on the countertop. It's this barbeque-chicken pizza recipe I found online, except I added pineapple. It sounds crazy, but I'm thinking it'll taste really good.

Then I run upstairs and jump into the shower to wash off all the volleyball sweat and sand from this morning. When I come out, Becca's pretty much unpacked her entire room into mine.

"What is all this stuff?" I rub my hair between the two ends of my towel as I take in the nail polish bottles and compacts and makeup brushes and something that looks like a tiny torture device and curling irons and a flat iron and the clothes and . . . exactly how much do you need to look nice?

"Oh, you know, makeover things!" Becca stands in the middle of it all, hands on her hips and beaming.

"But . . . there's so much of it."

"I like choices. Lots of choices. Eek! What are you doing to your hair? Halt! Right now! You'll give yourself split ends!"

I don't exactly know how else to towel dry my hair, but I stop anyway. Becca's already picked up a hair dryer and brush, like she can't wait to start.

"Um, I need to go put the pizza in the oven first." I toss my towel onto the only free space left in my room—the back of my desk chair—and fly downstairs, leaving Becca rolling her eyes behind me.

I pop the pizza in the oven and set the timer. Then I peer out the huge window in the breakfast nook. The sun is super bright, and the waves are crashing onshore. Perfect for surfing. Maybe I should just hang up this makeover idea and go to the beach. Lance and the other guys'll probably be out there. If Lance will even talk to me, that is. He's been acting bizarre since the party. In fact, he was even all weird this morning at the game, mumbling whenever I said anything to him and completely missing the ball when I sent it toward him. Whatever it is, I wish he'd get over it, or our team's gonna finish at the bottom of the heap.

Also, I might be having second thoughts about the makeover. I liked the way I looked at Linney's party (minus that awful dress), but I really, *really* wasn't okay with how everyone stared at me. I just want to look like maybe I'm not always headed to volleyball. I know I'm supposed to be Vi the Sporty Girl, but sometimes I want to be regular Vi. And who says regular Vi can't have nice hair and nails done in cotton-candy pink every once in a while without people making a big deal out of it?

"Vi! Come on, already!" Becca's voice calls from the stairs.

I guess there's no getting out of it now. I drag myself back up to my room, where Becca directs me to my desk, pointing at the mirror she's set up. She pats my hair with the towel (like that's actually going to dry it), and then attacks it with this huge flat-looking brush. Once the tangles are out, she switches on the dryer and brushes my hair while she dries it.

I'm still really curious about why she's here, doing my hair, instead of dragging me out to wherever Ryan is today so she can get more flirting in. So when she turns off the dryer, I ask.

"So . . . what's going on with Ryan?"

Becca sets the dryer down and puts on a smile that I'm guessing is fake. "Hey! I know! Let's talk about Lance and how he so completely, obviously, adorably likes you."

My face goes bright red in the mirror. "He does not like me. Not like that. We're friends." I think. I hope.

"Puh-lease." Becca flips my hair this way and that, making faces at it in the mirror. "He took one look at you at Linney's party and it was like a scene out of the movies. His eyes fell out of his head."

"They did not."

"Then why are you letting me do this, hmm? I know it's not just because you're bored on a Saturday afternoon." Becca drops my hair and grabs a big plastic box from my bed. She plugs it in and flips open the top, showing a row of curlers—just like the ones Lauren's Bubby had in her hair right before the dog party.

"Um . . . I'm not sure about curlers," I say.

"Hot rollers," she corrects me. "Trust me, your hair will look so super cute when I'm done with it. And you never answered the question."

I'm about to call her out on not answering mine either when—

Beep beep beep.

Saved by the pizza bell.

"Be right back." I race downstairs and pull the super-yummy-looking pizza from the oven. Normally I'd wait for it to cool a little before slicing, but I can just picture Becca dragging those curler things down here and snapping them into my hair if I don't hurry up.

I slice the pizza, slip the whole thing onto a big plate, and take it upstairs.

"That smells soooo good." Becca reaches for a slice, but I slap her hand away.

"It's hot. Wait for a moment."

"Whatevs. More time for *you* to answer my question now. Also, sit. Hot rollers wait for no man."

Ugh. I kinda hoped she'd forgotten she'd asked it. "I don't know . . ." I sit down and squirm a little in my chair. "I guess I liked the way I felt walking down the runway. Not the way everyone stared at me, because that was weird. But how I felt . . . pretty. I guess."

"There's nothing wrong with feeling pretty," Becca says.

"I just like having choices, you know? I don't always want to be the girl in the ponytail and flip-flops. Sometimes I want to look different. But sometimes I don't."

It feels really weird saying this stuff out loud, but

Becca's nodding like she completely understands.

"People aren't all one way or another," she says. "Variety is the milk of life. Or something. Like yesterday, I didn't do anything with my hair. I only dried it and put it back in a headband."

She's so earnest that I don't have the heart to tell her that that's way more than I do with my hair most days.

"Now watch what I'm doing so you can do it yourself. And don't tell me you don't have any hot rollers, because I'm leaving these here." Becca plucks a curler, or hot roller, or whatever it is, out of the box and winds my hair around it. Over and over and over again until I have a head full of rolled-up hair. I look like a piece of cauliflower.

"Pizza time! Followed by makeup time!" Becca snags a slice for each of us. "Okay. This is seriously ah-mazing, Vi," she says, swallowing a bite. "Hold up! Omigosh, omigosh, omigosh! Guess who just had the best idea for RSVP? Moi! We can advertise your fantabulous cooking skills. Like set up a booth in the Visitor's Center with some samples, and give them out with flyers. Once people taste your food, they'll be coming up with excuses for parties left and right. Plus we can for sure charge more if we're supplying the food." Becca looks happier than she's seemed all day.

Which makes it really hard to burst her bubble. "Sorry, Becs. I'm not cooking for anyone besides my friends and my dad." I bite into the pizza, and it *is* pretty good. The pineapple was the perfect touch.

"But whyyyyyyyyyy? Wait. This doesn't have something to do with that sleepover a bazillion gazillion years ago and how Linney acted about your spaghetti, does it?"

I look down at the pizza slice in my hands. It does. But it sounds so babyish to admit that Linney got to me like that. So I lie. "No."

"Uh-huh. Well, think about it, okay? Pinkie swear? Because you've met me, right? I'm so not gonna quit bugging you about it until you acknowledge how totally and completely genius my idea is. Kind of like what I did with Lauren." Becca shoves the last of her pizza into her mouth and brushes the crumbs from her hands. Then she dances across the room and gathers up nail polish and makeup. And tweezers, which she aims at my eyebrows.

I duck out of reach. "What are you doing?"

"Tweezing your eyebrows."

"Um, no." That sounds beyond painful. Why would I want little hairs ripped out of my face?

Becca crosses her arms. "Come on, Vi. I promise it doesn't hurt . . . very much. And I won't do a whole lot. We just need to create a shape, that's all."

"A shape?" Really, I don't see anything wrong with eyebrows being eyebrow-shaped.

"Let me just do one, and then you tell me if I should stop, okay?"

"Okay, fine." I clasp my hands between my knees and close my eyes. Becca leans in close. There's a little tugging on one of my eyebrows followed by a pinprick feeling.

"Okay?" she asks.

I nod. It does hurt a tiny bit, but it's not too awful.

"There," Becca says after she finishes my other eyebrow. "Done. Now, nails!" She hauls out a bag filled with a rainbow of colors. I pick out a very pale pink (even though she tries to sell me on a glittery blue), and she gets to work.

Once I have fingers and toes tipped in pink, Becca breaks out the makeup. I try to take notes in my head as she dabs gloss onto my lips and brushes light brown powder across my eyelids. She takes the torture-looking thing and attaches it to my eyelashes.

"What are you doing?" I say around her wrist, which is right in front of my face.

"Curling your eyelashes. Trust me. This will make your lashes look ten times longer and your eyes look as big as an anime character's."

What she's describing sounds like some kind of freakish mutant person. She finishes with the torture machine and swipes at my eyelashes with a mascara wand.

"There. Perfect. Now pick out something to wear, and then we'll take your hair down." Becca caps the mascara, and I glance at the clothes lying around the room.

She's grouped them into outfits, complete with shoes (which are all mine, since our feet are completely different sizes) and a purse and jewelry. Becca is nothing but serious about fashion. Buster's lounging on a blue skirt that reminds me of the pretty blue dresses at Linney's party. I roll him off and pick up the skirt.

"That would look ridiculously fabulous with your coloring!" Becca gushes.

I hold it up to my waist (really carefully so I don't smudge my nails) and look in the mirror. The skirt comes about halfway down my thighs. Which makes sense since Becca's like four feet tall. Or, at least, that's how it feels when I stand next to her. "Um, no. Too short."

"What are you talking about? You wear running shorts all the time! They're the same length."

"That's different. Those are shorts. What about this?" I pick up a long yellow maxi dress.

"Try it on!" Becca hands me the white sandals she picked to go with the dress. The pair of sandals that Meemaw bought for me to wear to Dad's coworker's wedding last spring (Dad complained until Meemaw insisted they were an early birthday present). I've never worn them since.

I tug on the dress and stuff my feet into the sandals. They actually aren't too uncomfortable since they're flat. But no way are they as comfy as my flip-flops or running shoes.

"Vi! Omigosh, you look divine, *dah*-link! Eeeee! Let's get your hair down." She pushes me back to the chair and unrolls my hair. Bouncy blond curls bob around my face. It all feels so . . . girly. "Okay, now we just have to squick some of these apart." Becca separates the curls until I have a lot of bounciness bopping me in the nose and covering my eyes.

"I can't see," I say through the hair.

"Hang on a sec." Becca's rifling through a little bag. She pulls something out and starts gathering some of the hair out of my eyes. Then she slips in a big barrette with white shells glued to it, and fastens the barrette behind my head. "Voila! Stand up."

She drags me over to the full-length mirror on the back of my door. This sunshiny person with bouncy hair and huge eyes looks back at me. She's kind of . . . pretty.

"You're totally wearing this to Illumination Night next weekend, you know that, right?" Becca says.

"I'll never be able to do this myself, you know."

"It's not that hard, silly. You just need to make the time for it."

"I guess . . ."

"Really, I swear on Dread Pirate it isn't. Just start small. Like, maybe tomorrow, only put on mascara and lip gloss. Then add something else the next day. Easy peasy."

I start to bite my lip, but then think better of it. I don't want that shiny pink gloss all over my teeth. It can't be that hard to swipe on some lip gloss, right?

"Cross your heart and promise me you'll try? If I don't see longer eyelashes tomorrow, I'm coming over here and taking home all this stuff I'm leaving for you to use. And your surfboard. And probably all your flip-flops, too. So you better promise, or else." Becca raises her eyebrows.

"Okay, okay! I promise. But . . ." I turn away from the mirror so I'm facing her. "You have to promise me that you'll lay off the whole Vi-cooks-for-the-business thing."

"Nooooope . . . no can do."

"You know how you clearly don't want to talk about Ryan? That's how I feel about this cooking thing." I twist the ends of my hair, and it takes Becca all of a half second to swat my hand away from my head.

Becca sighs likes I'm asking her to keep the secret of the century. "Fine. You win. But can I take some of that pizza home?"

"Knock-knock. Vi?" Dad's voice comes from the other side of my door.

I reach over and pull it open, and Dad peeks his head in.

"Is Becca staying—wow." Dad pulls off his Tar Heels cap, runs his hand through the sandy-brown hair plastered to his head, and then pulls the hat back on. Like that's going to make him see better. "Wow."

"Um, thanks?" I kind of wish people would stop staring at me when I look different than usual. It's not like I've turned into someone else. I'm still Vi. Just with a dress and bouncy hair.

"No, sweetie, I meant . . . wow. You really clean up." Now Dad's face is all red, like I'm sure mine is.

"Okay, thanks," I say again.

"But you know you can't go out with all of that . . . stuff on your face."

"*Dad*, please." I'll be lucky if I can even get the lip gloss on right. I turn to Becca. "I think Dad wanted to know if you were staying for dinner. I'm making chicken stir-fry."

"That's really nice, Mr. Husky," Becca says. "But I have to get home." When we were little, Becca couldn't ever say my last name, Alberhasky. It always came out like Alberhusky. Dad thought it was hilarious, and started calling himself Mr. Husky, and the name kind of stuck.

"Well, I have some great news to share," Dad says.

Becca and I look at each other. I twist the ends of one bouncy curl, and Becca doesn't even stop me. Dad's good news isn't always good news. Once, it was him scoring a bag of cheap clothes from the Church of the Victorious and Forgiving Holy Redeemer's yard sale, only for me to open it and find out they were all Linney's castoffs. Another time, the good news was him being interviewed by Channel 8 Wilmington about the union strike he was on and how hard it was for families to put food on the table during the strike.

So I'm not really sure I want to hear his good news right now.

But he's grinning like crazy, and Dad's smile always makes me smile. Even if I'm dreading what he's going to say. So I smile back and wait for it.

"I got a new job!"

"What! Really?" I fling my arms around him.

"Awesomesauce, Mr. Husky," Becca says. "Where?"

"I'm making a career change," Dad says. "Getting out of construction and going into maintenance. And the best part is . . . I'll be working at Sandpiper Beach Middle School!" He grins even wider.

"You're . . . what?" Did he say Sandpiper Beach Middle School? Like, *my* school?

"I'll be working at your school, sweetie," he says. "Isn't that great?"

I can't say anything.

"That's excellent news," Becca says. Except the look she gives me shows that she's super glad it's my dad coming to work at school and not one of her parents. "And you're gonna do maintenance? Is that like fixing up the school?"

"Sort of," Dad says. "Handyman stuff, and general cleaning duties."

"Like the janitor?" I feel completely numb as I talk.

"Well, yeah, that's one word for it. It doesn't pay a lot more, but it's steady work. No more waiting to see what the weather does."

"That's . . . great." I plaster a smile on my face, even though my stomach is sinking down, down, down to my pink toes in their white sandals.

Dad, working at my school, cleaning up my classmates' messes. This can't be happening.

Linney will eat me alive.

Sadie

13

TODAY'S TO-DO LIST:
- [ ] practice using grill lighter
- [ ] print out beach quote on paper disks
- [ ] hang fairy lights on front porch

"Vi, do you see where I put the other box of candles?" I ask, rooting through my garage for the plastic tub marked ILLUMINATION NIGHT. We only have two hours to put the paper disks around all the candles and set up the tables before the fish fry starts, and no way, nohow am I gonna be late to that.

"I'm on it," she answers, poking her head out from between two beach umbrellas and a wagon. I'm glad I talked Vi into hanging out with me today. She's been sort of mopey since she found out her dad's gonna be a janitor at our school this fall. I totally get it, but I can't help being a tiny bit jealous that he's taking jobs to be closer to her while my mom's jobs only seem to send her farther away. Vi hasn't really talked about it that much with me, though, and I think it's because she feels bad complaining about her dad when she knows I'd give anything to have mine alive.

Especially on Illumination Night.

Sometimes it's a hassle to live on a tiny island forty-five minutes from the closest mall. Other times (well, most times, really) I wouldn't trade it even for an apartment in the Eiffel Tower. And I *for sure* wouldn't trade it on Illumination Night. Today I don't even care that we haven't booked any more parties, even though we've been working like crazy on new ways to get the word out (like taking out an ad in the back of the *Sandpiper Beach Daily Gazette*), because it's *Illumination Night*.

Illumination Night is the last Friday in July every year and it's kind of like Christmas. In July. Except just with lights, not like, presents or plastic lawn reindeer or anything.

According to a brochure the Visitor's Center puts out, Illumination Night started way back in the 1940s as a way to give Christmas in July to a group of hometown boys from the island who were drafted into World War II and would be in France or Italy or Japan when December rolled around. Now it's just a purely fun tradition. Practically the whole town and all the weeklies meet up at seven in the town square for a giant fish fry, and there's always a band playing in the gazebo and the old people and little kids dance on the grass or under the statue of Merlin.

Just as soon as the sun sets, we run home to switch on our light displays and then the entire crowd strolls (or bikes, or scooters, or skateboards—no one drives unless they want to go five miles an hour and get nonstop dirty looks) around the streets and checks out the houses all lit up. Well, except for the houses right on the beach, because if any sea turtles hatched on Illumination Night, they'd head right for the twinkly strands instead of using the moon's light to guide them back to the ocean, which would be totally terrible. It's basically the only day of the year the people who live beachside are jealous of the townies!

I pretty much have the best of both worlds because I live right across from Pirate's Cove, which is tucked around a corner from the rest of the ocean, with only a tiny sandy beach and the rest rocks, so the turtles don't lay eggs there. Plus it's protected from the wind. Which means our cove gets to host the very best part of Illumination Night: the beach candles.

Every year, Izzy and I set up two folding tables at the entrance to the cove and we hand out hundreds of white taper candles slipped through round paper circles to catch the drippy wax. Mom always prints some quote about summer or the beach on the paper disks. Like, for instance, this year it's one by e.e. cummings that goes, *"for whatever we lose (like a you or a me) / it's always our self we find in the sea."*

Then people walk up the path to the beach, light their candles, and place them in the sand. By the end of the night, there are hundreds and hundreds of little flames there.

It's magical.

Becca, Vi, Lauren, and I always arrange ours like a heart, and sometimes people try to spell out words with theirs.

This year, instead of handing out the candles with Izzy, I actually get to be on the beach lighting them because Mom says I'm finally responsible enough to use the long grill lighter without getting burned. I have to bite my tongue to ask her how she knows this because it's not like she's come to any of my parties, and she's been so busy with a slew of new clients that she's barely even home for dinner most nights. But whatever. I'm totally not getting in a bad mood about her and ruining Illumination Night.

"I found all your dad's old fishing stuff. Would it be near that?" Vi asks. I can only see hints of her curlier-than-usual ponytail through the metal shelving unit.

I swallow the lump in my throat. It's been three years now, and even though we have pictures of Dad in almost every room of our house, most of his stuff has been donated or put in the attic, so it's not like a constant reminder of how he isn't around to wear the barn jacket in the coat closet. But Mom hasn't gotten to the garage yet, so there are Dad traps everywhere.

I sigh. It's like there's a bad-mood conspiracy going on today. And bad moods are totally not allowed on Illumination Night. (Which, FYI, was also Dad's favorite night of the year. Which, FYI, could also be the reason my bad mood is lurking in the first place.)

"You know what? Let's just bike over the bridge to Whitemore's Hardware and grab some new candles. I bet most of the leftover ones are stubby anyway."

Vi peers around the shelf. "Sounds good to me. I'll treat to lemon pops."

Whitemore's keeps a tiny freezer in the back with Popsicles for customers' kids. I make a face at Vi because we both know the Popsicles are free. She grins back.

"Are you looking for these?" My sister, Izzy, stands in the doorway to the garage and dangles two candles from her hands.

"What? Brat! Were you hiding those on purpose?"

Izzy squints at me. "Noooo. Geez. Why do you always jump to the worst conclusion? I was trying to help by getting started early; I already have thirty done."

Oh. Oops. Stupid bad mood.

"Sorry, Iz. I'm kind of in a funk today," I mumble, shooting Vi a guilty look.

"On Illumination Night?" my sister asks, wide-eyed. We follow her around to the side yard, where she's already got a candle-papering operation under way.

With Izzy's help, we knock out the rest in record time and drag the tables into place by the entrance to the cove. We hang a handmade DO NOT DISTURB sign on the tables and rush back to our houses to get changed into sundresses (yes, even Vi—color me amazed) for the fish fry.

Of course, Mom's still not home. She's been needing to scout a potential wedding location, and she had to wait for a day there would be a ceremony so she could see it all set up. But there's a text from her saying she'll meet us there later.

"Do you think the Romitos will have any new ones this year?" Izzy asks as we walk toward the square.

I laugh. After our beach candles and the Berrys' (who serve slices from a giant sheet cake in their driveway), the Romitos' get the biggest crowds. Most houses hang tiny white fairy lights, or globe lights like the ones restaurants sometimes use for their outside areas. Some people line their porch railings with votive candles under hurricane glasses.

But not the Romitos.

They have a crazypants collection of lights that grows by the year. Like strands of lit chili peppers, or beach umbrellas, or miniature poodles, or Volkswagen vans. Last year's additions were Hawaiian hula dancers and a strand of Easter egg–shaped lights. It's to the point now where some of the tourists who come every year will bring ones from their own cities to donate to the Romitos' collection. Their display is also my meeting spot with the girls if we haven't found each other by then, and we always have to budget at least twenty minutes to make sure we see every strand. I basically love it.

I love everything about Illumination Night.

We find Lo, Becs, and Vi (who really is wearing a dress and has let her curly hair out of its ponytail, although none of us have the heart to tell her she missed curling a few spots in the back because we don't want to discourage her) before the fish fry even starts this year. We chow down, then watch the little girls twirl around and around and the old people do old-timey dance steps. It's just as fun as ever. Plus the Romitos have tiny guitar lights on a strand, which Becca oohs and aahs over.

So far, so perfect. My bad mood fades as fast as the sun does.

Izzy and I have to run ahead to get in place before people start to make their way over to the cove. Since I'll be on the beach, she's supposed to have her friend Morgan helping her give out candles, but when we get there it's just us and another text from Mom. Running late. Who ever heard of so many wedding dramas? I can't even believe she'd miss Illumination Night. The parties are one thing, but Illumination Night? It's practically a holiday.

"Iz, I'll help you as long as I can, but I have to light

the candles on the beach. Can't you call Morgan and see where she is?"

"No way will she be home."

"Just try. Please, Izzy. It's my first year lighting the candles."

I hand her my cell phone and listen to Izzy's side of the conversation, which consists of a lot of "Oh, nos." This can't be good. Izzy hits end and hands my phone back to me, saying, "Morgan's sick."

"What?"

"Her mom said she started throwing up right before dinner." Izzy shrugs. "She was fine at camp this morning."

I look around helplessly. "But . . . but people are gonna be here any minute and I have to be on the beach. Except I can't leave you alone out here."

"I bet you could ask one of the grown-ups to use the lighter."

"That's not the point. It's finally my job and I want to do it," I whine.

"Well, you don't have to get mad at me. It's not my fault Morgan's sick."

Plus Mom's not here. Both of us are thinking it, even if neither of us says it.

"Fine. I'll call the girls to help. I don't know if they're allowed to use the lighter, but at least they can sit with you."

"I don't want the girls to sit with me. I want you."

"Izzy, don't be a baby. I'm trying to get a job done here."

"That's what you've been saying all summer," Izzy mumbles under her breath, but I catch it.

Whatever. She's only ten. She totally doesn't understand how much work—fun work, but still—it can be to run a company.

My phone buzzes and I check it. "Lo just texted me back. She's right around the corner, and Vi and Becca are stopping off for a piece of cake, then heading straight over too."

Izzy just shrugs and slumps in her seat. We sit in silence while we wait.

An hour later I've come to the realization that Mom and Dad exaggerated the importance of this job when they did it. I got to light the first few, but then everyone just turned to the person behind them and lit one candle off the other, so I'm entertaining myself by relighting any that have blown out. The beach is covered in tapers stuck into little hills of sand that people used to prop them up. Between their flickering, the water shimmering in the moonlight, and the blinking stars, it's like one giant twinkle party out here.

Off to one side a few of the kids from the high school built a bonfire, but they got bored and left it. A bunch of my classmates swooped in and claimed it and now someone is strumming a guitar. The fire smells like summer nights.

"Sades!" Becca gathers the skirts of her maxi dress in her hands and carefully takes a giant step over a circle of candles to stand beside me. "Do you ever get that feeling where everything is so perfect and you're so totally happy to be exactly where you are that it makes you sad, but you can't explain why?"

I really, really do.

We're quiet for a few seconds and then Becca squints over at the bonfire.

"Who's on the guitar?"

She, Lauren, and Vi have been taking turns helping Izzy, so she hasn't watched any of the action on the beach. I follow her eyes. "Actually, um, I think it might be Ryan."

"Oh." If Becca's surprised, she doesn't show it.

"Do you want to go over there?"

"Nah."

Now I try to hide *my* surprise. I mean, I know she's been really mellow about Ryan since we had our talk the other week, but I figured that would change once we were face-to-face with him.

I'm about to protest when Lance calls out to us. He must have noticed us staring at them. "Hey, y'all! Come on over!"

I wave at him and grab Becca's hand.

"C'mon, we'll just say hi." She looks like she wants to protest, but she doesn't say anything, just follows me. When we reach the group, everyone says hi and we drop to the sand. "Hey. Are you taking requests?" I ask.

Ryan laughs. "I'm not good enough to know whole songs yet."

Then he glances up, sees Becca beside me, and promptly ducks his head.

Poor Becs. I know she's halfway mortified thinking back on how she's been acting around Ryan, even though she doesn't have to be. She's really quiet (soooo not like Becca) while the rest of us chat softly and Ryan picks at strings.

After about twenty minutes I hear my name being called and spot Lauren waving at the beach entrance. I stand and brush sand off the backs of my legs, then reach out a hand to tug Becca up. We only get two steps before Becca says, "Hang on. I just need to tell Ryan something."

Oh, no. This can't be good. Either she's gonna be all flirty, which is pretty counterproductive at this point, *or* she's gonna apologize or something, which would be worse, considering about a quarter of the seventh grade is hanging out at the bonfire and would overhear it.

But before I can stop her, she's crouching in the sand next to Ryan. He looks resigned, like he couldn't believe she'd left him alone as long as she had, but it's not normal flirty Becca who says, "Hey." This Becca's soft and quiet. "I just wanted to let you know your low E is out of tune. Also, when you're playing your open chords, you're not playing on the very tips of your fingers, so some of the notes are getting lost. Just move your wrist forward and roll up to the tips and you'll solve it."

Then she straightens, jogs in the sand a few steps to catch up to me, and tucks an elbow through mine.

I don't want to chance glancing back at Ryan, but I definitely don't hear any music as we walk away, so I'm thinking he's probably got his jaw hanging open.

But I don't even have a chance to mention that to Becca, because Lauren's waving with both hands now. Only she's not smiling.

We have to weave through candles, so I can't run. "What's wrong?"

"It's Izzy. I think she's sick!"

We pick our way across the rest of the beach as fast as we can, then follow Lauren down the path to Cove Street, where the tables are set up. As soon as we come over the little hill, I see Izzy clutching her stomach. Vi's offering her sips from a water bottle.

"Iz?" I race up to her and put my hand on her arm. "What's up?"

She looks at me and a tear slips down her cheek.

Vi speaks instead. "She just completely puked in the grass over there. I offered to take her to lie down, but she said she only wanted you."

"I don't feel so good, Sade." Izzy sounds terrible.

I share a glance with the other girls and put my arm around my sister.

"We'll take care of the candle cleanup," Lauren

offers immediately. The others nod enthusiastically.

"Don't worry about a thing. We'll handle it," Vi says. She's already pulling her new curls into a ponytail holder and knotting the bottom of her dress at the knees.

I give them grateful smiles, then walk my sister gingerly back to the house, where I tuck her into cool sheets and place a damp washcloth on her forehead.

"I'm sorry, Iz. You probably caught whatever Morgan has," I say.

"I got sick in front of your friends!" This time tears are streaming down Izzy's face. I gape at her.

"So *what*? Like they care. Geez, Iz, you're sick. You can't help that. No one cares, I promise."

"No one does care!" Izzy says with a giant sniffle. "Not you, not Mom. Neither of you are ever around when I need you. You're both too busy with your dumb businesses."

Wait a second, wait a second, wait *one second*. *Mom* is always busy with *her* dumb business. I mean, yeah, I have RSVP, but we haven't even had a job in two weeks and before that we were . . .

Kind of busy. Not the whole time, but I guess even the times we didn't have actual parties, we were meeting up at the *Purple People Eater* to plan them or getting stuff we needed together. And the last two weeks have been all about drumming up new business. So yeah, I guess I was busy, but it was a fun kind of busy and I was with my friends, so it didn't feel anything like Mom's kind of busy. Besides, Mom uses her job as an excuse for everything, and she's way worse because *she* has other responsibilities. Like TWO KIDS.

I'm not missing out on anything *I'm* supposed to be doing, even when I have a million party-planning things to do. It's summer. I don't even have homework. I basically have zero responsibilities.

Except being a good big sister to Izzy. Dad made me cross-my-heart promise before he died.

I glance at Iz. She's slumped back against her pillow and her eyes are closed. It's like finally getting that off her chest took the last strength she had.

I watch her chest move up and down but really I'm in my head, replaying a bunch of times when Izzy wanted to help us or hang out and I ignored her calls or sent her away.

Izzy's breathing gets soft next to me and I think she's fallen asleep. But I just lie there in her bed, thinking.

Am I just like Mom?

GREAT SCOTS! ONE OF OUR OWN IS MOVING TO THE HIGHLANDS!

Please join us in wishing a bonny fare-thee-well to

Mr. Charles Vernon

On Saturday, August 8, at five o'clock

Sandpiper Active Senior Living, 1101 Rosalinde Street

Wear your finest Scottish attire and get ready to dance

a bagpipe jig in honor of our beloved friend!

Your fond memories are the only gifts Mr. V needs

Hosted by Mrs. Geraldine "Bubby" Simmons

RSVP to Sadie Pleffer at (910) 555-0110 or

sadie@rsvpmail.com

14

Lauren

camaraderie noun \käm(ə)ˈrädərē\
a feeling of mutual trust and friendship among
persons in a group
Use in a sentence:
I enjoy the camaraderie I share with Vi, Sadie, and
Becca, even when we're chasing runaway dogs,
wearing puffy old-fashioned dresses, and shopping
at (ugh) Party Me Hearties.

*Z*ach! Let's GO, already. I have a ton of stuff to do
before I have to be back at the marina this afternoon."
I give his bedroom door a good kick. Maybe too good
of a kick, because I forgot I was wearing flip-flops and
ended up whacking the hard wooden door with my
bare toes. I hop up and down as I wait for him to answer.

"Go. Away."

So I pound with my fist. "You promised you'd drive me over to the library."

"Take the golf cart and leave me alone."

"Jerk!" I give the door one last good thump, and turn on my heels toward the garage. Why do I get stuck with the lazy brother who can't get up in time to drive me to the other end of the island? I mean, it's not like it's the crack of dawn or anything. It's ten o'clock. But considering I was woken up by music blasting from his room at three a.m., I guess I shouldn't be surprised he's still asleep.

I pull out of the garage just as Mom drives in. She rolls down her window and blinks at me with bleary eyes. She got called into emergency surgery last night, which ended up taking hours. Her curly hair is starting to frizz, and she runs a hand over it as she asks, "Where are you going?"

"Party errands."

"Can't you ask Zach to drive you?"

"Zach is still asleep. I've been up since seven." I decided a long time ago that the most successful people get up early every day, even on weekends. Mom's always asking me if I get enough sleep, but if I'm going to do better than Zach or Josh, then sleep can wait.

"Then what about your bike?" Mom asks.

"Too much to carry," I say as I twist the seashell key ring hanging from the ignition of the golf cart. "And I have to go to the library."

"The library? That's way over by the cove." Mom's eyebrows knit together, and I'm sure she's picturing me splatted out in front of Sadie's house or something.

"It's fine, Mom. It's not that far away. And I promise to stay on the side streets."

She sighs. "I wish your dad never bought those carts, but all right. Be careful."

"Of course," I tell her before I roll on down the driveway. I'm going to hit the library first to rent some movies, and then the bank to finally deposit the money I made on Bubby's dog birthday party, and last of all Marks Makes Cakes, since Vi flat out refuses to set foot in there again. What I really should be doing is a marathon read of the last two books on my summer reading list, but Sadie's been staying home with Izzy all week, so without me, it would've been just Becca and Vi getting everything ready.

Because we *finally* booked another party. I don't know if "booked" is the right word, since even though Becca's been chatting up every single weekly who comes into the Visitor's Center, and Vi made this awesome page full of pictures and captions from the parties we've already done to include with the flyers, and Sadie's been making calls to everyone we know who has a birthday coming up this month, no one's actually booked us for anything. Until last night, when I got a text from Bubby.

Lo baby, my life iz over!

Since she's seventy-two years old, when she says something like that, I kind of picture her in the hospital. *What happened? Where are you?* I typed back.

My apt. But I'm sooooo sad! Mr. V is moving on.

Mr. V is in the hospital?

Nooooo . . . wish he wuz tho b/c then I'd still have a chance w/ him, she wrote.

What are you talking about?

He's moving 2 Scotland!

Ohhhhh . . .

And that's when Bubby had the bright idea that if Sandpiper Active Senior Living (meaning her) threw Mr. Vernon a going-away party, then he might notice her and realize how wonderful she is and change his mind.

Guess who she wanted to plan the party?

So I know I should be grateful that we have another party. It just feels as if it doesn't count because Bubby is my family. That's like if you paint some amazing work for the elementary-school charity art auction, feel all proud about it hanging up in the school gym, and then your mother buys it. (And yes, that happened. May second, three years ago. The painting is still hanging in our living room. It's practically the only non-boat thing in the room.)

I roll into the square (careful to look in all directions just in case Mom's stats on golf-cart crashes are correct), and then turn right, around Merlin and the gazebo and toward Lava Java and the bridge.

"Lo! Wait!" Becca comes running from the Visitor's Center, her sparkly red purse flying out behind her.

I pull over in front of Lava Java and wait for Becca.

"Whew! I'm *so* glad you're here. I have to go to the photo counter at the pharmacy to print these pictures for the collages. Our printer's dead and Dad's using the one at the Visitor's Center to print out a gazillion and two flyers about the Founder's Day stuff next month. Plus I have to buy all the stuff to make the collages. So where are you going?" Becca leans on the golf cart and waits for me to answer.

"The library first." I check the time on my phone. Ten fifteen. I have to move if I'm going to make it to all my stops and back across the island to the marina before noon.

"Awesomesauce. We can stop at the pharmacy on the way." She slips into the passenger seat of the golf cart and tucks her purse between her feet. And then looks at me, like she can't figure out why I'm not driving yet.

"Um, no. I can't drive friends, remember?" I wait for her to get out, but she doesn't budge.

"C'mon, Lauren! You're a really, really good driver, and the pharmacy isn't that far away. And besides, how am I supposed to carry all those pictures and glue and construction paper and markers on my bike? Pleeeeease?" She widens her eyes and blinks them, like she's going to cry big, fat tears if I don't agree.

"I can't, I'm sorry. If my parents see, I'll be dead."

"Your dad's at the marina, right?"

"Yes. He's got some contractors coming at eleven to look at replacing part of the dock."

"And your mom is . . ."

"Home. She was up all night at the hospital." Wait. I see where she's going with this, and I fell right into it.

"So how in the world are your parents going to see

235

us riding around if we don't go anywhere near your house or the marina?" Becca straightens her shoulders, lifts her chin, and gives me her best toothy grin.

"Ugh . . . you know I hate it when you do this." I grip the steering wheel and try to figure out how to get Becca out of the golf cart.

"What? Letting your BFF finally ride in this seriously ah-mazing set of wheels? Giving all you've got to our business? Driving past cute guys with our hair flying in the wind?" Becca's already scanning the square for boys.

"No, breaking the rules. And this thing only goes about twenty miles an hour, so not much is going to be flying in any wind."

"I promise I'll give you all the rides you want in my future cherry-red convertible. Now, let's go." Becca pulls a pair of big sunglasses and a filmy-looking white scarf from her purse. She ties the scarf around her head, puts on the sunglasses, and then sits there like some kind of black-and-white movie star.

"Right," I say, as I shake my boring, non-scarfed, non-sunglassesed head and aim the golf cart around the square.

"Hi, Linney!" Becca gives Linney, who's just coming

out of Lava Java, a little finger wave, just like you see beauty queens do in parades.

"Becca! Shh!" I hit the gas pedal to try to move a little faster.

"What? You know we're totally making Linney jealous. I can't wait to tell Vi."

And Linney might tell her mom, who might tell my mom. I just want to go to the library and get this over with.

"What exactly is Vi up to? I thought she was doing the collages and you were in charge of getting food from the deli," I say as we roll down Live Oak Drive, past the little souvenir and fudge shops.

"Oh, that." Becca giggles. Which is super annoying. I hate it when I don't know what's going on.

"What's going on?" I demand.

"I thought that if Vi was in charge of food, she'd see how she could make something so much more yummy than anything she can get at the deli. I wouldn't be surprised at all if she decided to make all the food at our next party. Hey, look, there's Lance and his mom. Hey, can we stop? Hiiiii, Lance!" Becca gives him her movie-star wave as we slowly roll by Terrific Teeth, the only dentist's office around.

"We can't stop. Too much to do. And before you ask, no, we are *not* doing a Ryan drive-by either."

Becca ducks her head to study her lap. Hmm. Strange.

"What's up? Are you over Ryan or something?"

"Or something," Becca says, and her voice sounds kind of funny.

"What did I miss?"

"Nothing, why?" Now she sounds a little defensive. "Everything's fine. Seriously. Just yesterday he came into the Visitor's Center looking for a place to buy paint for his aunt's shed and I wrote him out directions to White-more's. No biggie."

"And then you offered to lend your incredible eye for design in helping him pick out paint colors, of course, right?"

Becca punches me in the arm. "Very funny." She tilts her head. "Although I really *do* have an eye for color." She shakes her head. "But nah."

I take my eyes off the road for just a millisecond and glance sideways at her. "Where is my Becca and when can I see her again?"

Becca giggles. "Don't be a dork. Okay, new subject. If we can't stop and talk to anyone, can we at least find some tunes? Does this thing have a place to plug in my phone? I have a new playlist on it. You'll lo-ove."

"Becca, it's a *golf* cart. I think you're supposed to be quiet on a golf course. Hey, you know how you could be helpful? Quiz me with the flash cards in my backpack."

Becca makes a face. "No way. This is called having fun, Lo. Enjoy it already."

Right. Fun. I can do this.

But okay. I admit the parties are fun. Not the driving around to stores with an illegal (according to the Rules By Mom) passenger or going to bakeries owned by the mother of the snootiest girl in town, but the actual parties with my friends.

I'm completely worn out from running all over the place in the golf cart with Becca and then working the afternoon at the marina, so I'm ready to at least try to relax and have fun when I open the door to the party room at Sandpiper Active Senior Living that evening. Then I see Bubby.

"Becca!" I snag her sleeve as she's arranging the photo collages she made on a table. "Can you talk some sense into Bubby? Did you see what she's *wearing*?"

Becca shrugs. "I think she looks cute."

That's when I realize that Becca and Bubby are pretty much dressed the same: red plaid skirt that looks like a kilt, white button-down top, and a little hat with a pom-pom. The only difference is that Becca has her red hair in two braids sticking out from under her hat, and Bubby's hat rests on overcurled white hair.

"Okay. All right." *Just breathe, Lauren. Who cares what they're wearing? It's a Scotland-themed party, after all.* And then I see Sadie, who's got on a green plaid skirt and matching pom-pom hat.

Sadie spies me and zooms over. "Lauren, why aren't you dressed up?"

"I didn't realize we had to do the kilt thing too. I thought that was just for the guests."

Sadie shakes her head and sighs, like I'm completely and utterly hopeless at throwing parties with silly themes.

"Look." I hold up the bags I'm carrying. "I brought a cake with the Loch Ness monster on it, bagpipe-shaped cutouts to hang up, and some movie with Mel Gibson called *Braveheart*. I had to make these cutouts, you know. It's not like anyplace in Sandpiper Beach sells bagpipe cutouts." Skull-and-crossbones cutouts, yes.

Lighthouse cutouts, definitely. But bagpipes? No way.

"Perfect. Now let me just put this on you so you don't look like you wandered into the wrong party." Sadie wraps a plaid sash diagonally over my shoulder and ties it at my waist. Becca's face turns a little green when she sees how awful the plaid goes with my pink shirt.

Sadie steps back, squints at me, and then pulls a pom-pom hat from a bag behind her. "You need a tam," she says.

"No, I—"

Becca takes the bags from my hands as Sadie slaps the tam on my head. I adjust the thing so it's not falling over my eyes. "Hey, do you think your mom will finally be able to make it today?" I ask.

"Nope." Sadie makes a face. "This one's my fault, though. Since I'm not working for her anymore, I keep forgetting to look at her wedding calendar. She's actually had a wedding on the books for today since last fall."

"Bummer," Becca says, her arms full of the stuff I brought.

"Sorry, Sades," I add.

"Yeah, well. It's still gonna be a great event, right?"

Sadie takes the movie and starts setting up the video equipment we borrowed from the Visitor's Center. Usually the TV shows a loop of *The Best of Sandpiper Beach and Surrounding Scenic Sandpiper County*. Becca makes an appearance in the background about halfway through, leading a tour as the Dread Pirate. She swears it's Pete, not her, but everyone can see her hair sticking out from under the pirate bandanna.

I'm standing there, wondering if I can talk Bubby into some normal clothes and whether I can get away with hiding my pom-pom hat behind the boxes of bingo cards on the nearest shelf, when I hear my name.

"Psst! Lauren!" Vi's calling me from the back door (aka the Great Dog Escape Door).

I push my hair forward to cover at least part of the plaid sash and go to help Vi. Who is also wearing a plaid skirt. Really. "Am I the only one who didn't get the message?" I ask.

"What?" She's only half paying attention to me, and then I see why. She's got the handle of a little red wagon in her hand, and the wagon is full of aluminum-foil-wrapped dishes.

And I'm completely stunned. Vi is such an amazing cook, but is totally shy about it. "Vi! Did you make all of this? What's in there? I can't wait to try it!"

"No! Geez, will everyone just lay off the cooking thing? This is from the deli." She bites her lip. "Okay, fine. I might've made some crab dip. It's in the cooler. But don't make a big deal out of it, all right?"

I can't help the smile that spreads across my face. "So you need help getting it in? I could've brought it in the golf cart, you know, so you didn't have to walk with it." I seriously cannot wait to try that dip. Maybe I can sneak some as we're setting up the food table. I'll have to grab some for Zach too. Crab dip is his absolute favorite. I can hold it hostage till he agrees to return the movie to the library for me.

"I only walked from the deli. Ms. Sanders next door let me borrow her kids' wagon and gave me a ride there on her way to pick up her son." Vi pulls the wagon in as I hold the door open.

As I help her unload and uncover the food, Vi keeps making comments like "Why didn't they offer a vegetarian stew?" and "Where's the haggis? How can you have a moving-to-Scotland party without serving haggis?" I want to tell her there'd be plenty of vegetarian stew and haggis (yuck) if she had made the rest of the food, but I stay quiet. Making crab dip for a big group of people is a huge step for Vi.

When everything's set up (and after I sneak a taste of the dip), I plop onto a chair in the corner to memorize vocab words while we wait for the guests to show up.

"What are Anna and McKenna doing here?" Sadie asks as I'm committing to memory the definition of "collaborate" (to cooperate or work together).

I shrug. "Maybe they're visiting their grandparents and got lost." I wave at Anna, who's on the It's All Academic team with me at school.

Sadie stops rearranging chairs that were perfect the first time. "They're dressed up."

Sure enough, Anna's got on a tartan skirt and McKenna looks like she's borrowed a huge plaid shirt from her dad. I put my flash cards down as they make their way over to us.

"This is the party, right?" Anna asks.

Sadie blinks at her. "Yeeesss . . ."

"See, I told you we'd be too early. Hey, there's food! I'm starving." McKenna zooms toward Vi and the food table.

"So . . . did your grandparents invite you?" It's the

only logical conclusion I can come to. Why else would two girls from our class show up at a senior's going-away party?

Anna laughs. "No, silly. Bubsters3000 invited us on Twitter. Who is she, anyway? Wait, are y'all throwing this party?" She tilts her head and studies me as if she's never seen me before. "Are *you* Bubsters3000?"

"No," I say with as much emphasis as possible.

"RSVP's doing the party," Sadie adds. "And I saw that invite from Bubsters3000, but I didn't pay attention to it since it was for the same day as this party. I didn't realize that it *was* this party. But how . . ."

"I'm pretty sure I know who Bubsters3000 is." I leave Sadie with Anna and march toward Bubby, who's talking with two older ladies who have just arrived.

"Maybe if I gave him a locket with a picture of me inside?" she's saying to her friends. "No, too old-school. How about a cell phone with an album full of my pictures?"

"Excuse me," I say. "Bubby, can I talk to you for a minute?"

"Of course, my Lo. See you gals later." Bubby waves at them with just the tips of her fingers, like she's a pageant queen. Or Becca in the golf cart.

When we're out of earshot, I leap right in. "Bubsters3000?"

Bubby giggles. "That's my Tweeter name. Aren't you following me?"

Is it horrible if you don't follow your own grandmother on Twitter? It's not like I really have time to check my feed. "It's Twitter, not Tweeter. And why are there girls from my class here?" And just as I ask that, I spot a group of guys near the door. I squint and realize they're Zach's friends. Becca's already welcoming them with extra tams. What in the world?

"Oh, them!" Bubby says with a wave of her hand. "I sent a Tweeter note to everyone I could find who had Sandpiper Beach in their profile." She puts her hands on her hips. "You'd know that if you followed me."

"But . . ." I gesture sort of uselessly at another bunch of kids coming through the door. "Why? I thought this was Mr. Vernon's party?"

"He's moving to be with his grandkids. I thought he'd appreciate having more than a bunch of oldsters at this hullabaloo. I need to go welcome them." Bubby gives me a grin and makes her way toward the closest group of girls. "Hey, yo, girlfriends!"

"Lauren?" Sadie grabs me by the arm. "What's going

on? We're not ready for this many people!"

"There's not enough food, that's for sure," Vi adds from behind Sadie.

Before I can answer, Becca jogs over to join us. "Lance said he got a Twitter invitation from someone named Bubsters3000. Everyone's saying that. Wait, how come *I* didn't get an invitation?" Her lower lip juts out like she's super sad about my grandmother not inviting her to a kilt-wearing old-people party.

"Lance is here?" Vi's face goes a little pale.

"It's Bubby," I tell them. "She went a little crazy and invited the whole town. On Twitter."

"Bubby's on Twitter, and I didn't know?" Becca says, like that's the most important thing I just said.

Sadie looks as if she's about to hyperventilate. Vi keeps throwing these worried glances at the food table. And Becca's practically bouncing on her toes, trying to see who else has arrived.

And what can we do? Nothing, that's what. Bubby wanted a giant party, and now she's got one. And all the seniors seem to be rolling with it. The two ladies Bubby was talking to earlier are chattering away with Anna and McKenna. But some of the kids don't look too sure. Zach's friends are grouped in a corner, and some sixth-grade girls are standing with their arms crossed and frowning like they just walked into math class instead of a party.

"We need to start, fast," I tell my friends. "Or Bubby's going to lose half her party."

"They've pretty much demolished the food," Becca says.

"Okay, let me think." Sadie presses her hands to either side of her face and surveys the crowd.

We're all quiet for a minute, until Vi pipes up.

"There's a kitchen here, right?" she asks.

"On the other side of the dining room." I point to the doors that lead from the party to the dining room.

"You're going to make something!" Becca claps her hands.

Vi turns red. "No, and there's not enough time anyway. I'm going to see if they have any snacks we can buy. Chips and salsa, that kind of thing. I know that isn't Scottish, Sades, but we need more food."

Vi runs off toward the kitchen and Sadie shoves some note cards into my hands. "Lauren, can you do the welcome? Becca, you try to gather everyone toward Lauren, and I'll go see if we have any music that isn't so . . . bagpipey."

"Wait . . ." I call after Sadie, but she's disappeared into the crowd with Becca. "Okay, well . . ." I climb up onto a chair and look at the note cards. "Excuse me?"

Everyone just keeps on talking. Where's Vi and her whistle when I need her? Luckily, Bubby spies me from across the room. She cups her hands to her mouth and yells, "Hey, my peeps! Hush up and listen to Lolo, already!"

The room goes silent, and everyone's staring at me.

Okay, this is uncomfortable. I check the first note card. "Welcome, everyone, to Mr. Vernon's going-away party!"

The seniors clap politely, and the kids just . . . look at me. I clear my throat and smile. "Och, ye ken Mr. Vernon is movin' to auld Scotland to be with his son and daughter-in-law and their wee bairns." Seriously? Who wrote this stuff? Why didn't Sadie give the cards to Becca, the actress-in-training? I can barely even read this. "Aye, so tonight we lads and lassies are goin' to have a belter of a good time!"

Someone hoots from the back of the room—one of Zach's friends, I think—and all the seniors join in.

I squint at the note card. What Sadie's written next doesn't even look like English. I shove the cards into my pocket and say in my normal voice, "Now Mr. V's friends can share their favorite memories."

The seniors move toward the chairs, and just in time, Vi arrives with a cartload of food. The kids head straight for the Jell-O cups and kosher dill pickles. That'll keep them busy for a little while, but we'll have to think of something else—soon. Sadie goes to rescue Vi, and Becca guides an elderly woman to a seat near Mr. Vernon.

I turn my attention to the seniors. Bubby nearly leaps out of her seat when I ask who wants to start.

"Oh, Mr. V," she says, fluttering her eyelashes. "I'll never forget when you came to the Moonlight Mix-It-Up and asked me to dance. Maybe we can reenact that tonight, hmm? I know all the latest moves."

Mr. Vernon coughs a little and squirms in his seat.

"Ohhhh . . . ," I hear Becca say just under her breath, right next to me.

"So, um, thanks, Bubby. Who's next?" I ask, really quickly before Bubby can say anything else.

A tall, thin man with barely any hair stands up. "Charlie, you remember when we were on that fishing excursion? You swore you'd catch the biggest mackerel, but hoooo boy, you couldn't catch much of nothing over three inches." The whole group, Mr. V. included, bursts into laughter.

"And then Ginny lost her lunch over the side, remember that?" one of the women says.

Becca grabs one of the photo collages off the table and hands it to Mr. Vernon. He starts laughing so hard, he can barely catch his breath. "Who took this picture?"

I peek over his shoulder and see the one in the middle of the collage. It's Mr. Vernon, proudly holding up the world's tiniest mackerel while a round little old woman leans over the side of the boat behind him. Another person—not in the shot—is giving him bunny ears. It reminds me of all the silly pictures I have of my friends.

"Thank you all for this," he says. "I'll never forget such a great group of folks."

As they continue to tell stories, I look around at my friends. Becca's laughing along with the seniors. Vi's making sure all the kids have something to eat. And Sadie catches my eye and gives me a thumbs-up.

I can't imagine moving to another country and leaving them behind. Who would listen to me complain about my brothers the way Sadie does? Without Vi, I'd have to collect shells by myself and eat store-bought pita chips. And Becca's always the one making me try new things.

But one day, I will move away. Not for a few years, and probably not to Scotland, but still. When that time comes, I won't have my best friends around to hang out in a dirty old yacht or light candles on the beach.

I get what Bubby was talking about now. And it makes me want to keep this moment going for as long as I can.

"Sadie couldn't find anything that wasn't Scottish," Becca says as we watch Sadie mute the movie on the Visitor's Center TV. "And it's not like this place has any kind of dock to play music from our phones."

"Bagpipes are better than nothing, I guess." The food's pretty much gone, and the kids are standing around like they're waiting for something to happen.

Some kind of jig blasts from the stereo. Becca and I push the chairs out of the way, and a group of the seniors, Bubby right in front, pulls Mr. Vernon to his feet. They jump right into dancing, laughing and talking the whole time.

But none of the kids move at all. Zach's friends are headed toward the door again. This isn't good. Not only would Bubby be upset that her party is a bust, but

RSVP's reputation won't be so great if everyone checks out early.

"What can we do?" Becca asks.

I'm racking my brains when the last person I expected to see at this party walks through the door.

Zach.

Great. Like I really want my brother here to witness this disaster of a party. I only have one idea, and it'll either save the whole thing or make me the laughingstock of Sandpiper Beach Middle School. I don't have time to lay out the pros and cons. I just have to do it—for Bubby, for my friends and RSVP, and for myself.

I yank the note cards from my pocket and toss them onto my backpack in the corner. "Let's dance!" I yell to Becca as I race through the jig-dancing seniors to grab Sadie and Vi.

"What are you doing? I don't know how to dance!" Vi gets this panicked look on her face.

"Neither do I! Who cares? Let's just have fun! And maybe save this party." I try to follow what the seniors are doing but end up stepping on Sadie's heels.

"Lauren, you are officially the worst bagpipe dancer ever!" Sadie says over the music.

"I know!" With that, I grab her hands and start spinning in a big circle. Everyone backs out of the way, clapping in time to the music. A lot of the kids have joined the group now, some of them clapping and others sort of staring at me. Which makes sense, since I'm not exactly the dance-in-the-middle-of-a-crowd kind of girl. But I think about Mr. Vernon moving away and about Bubby and Alma, and I don't care. Right now, I just want to have fun with my best friends.

"Go, Lo! Go, Sadie!" Becca yells.

We spin and spin and spin until we're laughing so hard and my pom-pom hat flies off and we're so dizzy that we fall in a heap on the floor.

"Lauren?" Zach's standing over me, holding out a hand. "What . . . what are you doing?"

I scramble up and do a little jig kind of move. Or what I think is a jig kind of move, since I've never really done one before. "Dancing! Come on!"

He blinks at me.

"Look, if I'm dancing, so can you. This is Bubby's party, so we owe it to her to make it good. If you dance, then maybe everyone else will too." My breath comes out all huffy, since I'm not really used to this much exercise.

Zach glances at his friends, and then he laughs. But

he's not laughing at me. "All right. But not to this . . . music. I've got a dock in my car."

I want to hug him, but that would be weird. So instead I tell him thanks. When he comes back and plugs in some normal music, the party really starts. I dance and dance and dance with my friends until it feels like my feet will fall off.

A little later, while Becca's having a heart-to-heart with Bubby (who's all distraught about Mr. V. leaving and how he hasn't gone for her Moonlight Mix-It-Up reenactment), I'm eating chip crumbs with Vi and Sadie when I feel someone over my shoulder. The seniors loved Vi's dip and have been coming up asking for the recipe all night. I pull out the pen for her to write it down again when the person speaks.

But it's not one of the seniors. Instead, it's a staff member from Sandpiper Active Senior Living. "Hi, girls. I was wondering if you had a card or anything? You see, my daughter wants this crazy birthday party and it's going to require a lot of energy and, well, you certainly seem to have that. And you look like you're having so much fun. Would you be interested in maybe planning her party?"

Sadie jumps out of her chair and hands the woman

our business card. "Of course! We'd love to."

"Great! I'll be in touch." The woman takes the card and leaves, and Sadie lets out a squeal. Then she looks at me.

"Thank you, Lauren."

"Um, for what?"

"For joining and actually having fun with it. And then working so hard to pull it off. I thought we were goners when all those kids from school showed up. But together, we figured it out. And I think you're the reason why that woman wants us to do her kid's party." Sadie throws her arms around me and Vi gives me a high five at the same time.

"Really?" Who knew that letting yourself go like that could actually make you look more professional?

"Absolutely. RSVP is back!"

So we celebrate by dancing, of course.

15

Becca

Daily Love Horoscope for Scorpio:
Falling stars aren't the only keepers of
wishes—you have more power than you
realize to make your dreams come true.

Who wants to check Wikipedia? Someone somewhere *has to* have figured out a way to get into a sleeping bag on the beach without filling the bottom with
enough sand to build a ginormous castle." I huff my hair
out of my eyes and dump my bag. Again.

Almost like the beach is laughing at me, the wind
shoots most of the sand straight back into my face.

Vi giggles. Of course, *she's* completely in her beachy
girl element. She probably brings sand in at night and

puts it in her bed on purpose so she can feel all at home while she sleeps.

Lauren and Sadie are on the other side of me, having the same epic battle with nature.

Le sigh.

This had better be worth it.

"This is gonna be so worth it," Sadie says, almost like she read my mind. "I can't believe all our parents signed off on this."

"Well, now that Vi's living right here, it's really no different than when we have sleepovers in our yards," says Lauren.

"Yeah, except instead of sharing a fence with cranky old Mr. Nelson, Vi gets to share her backyard with dolphins," Sadie says.

"And sand," I mumble, tossing my bag into a crumpled heap. I give up.

But, secretly, I really do think it will be worth any amount of scratchy sand in between my toes tonight. Because, for the first time ever, our parents are letting us stay out all night on the beach to watch the Perseid meteor shower.

The meteor shower—also known as the Night of a Gazillion Shooting Stars, also *also* known as the

Night of a Gazillion *Wishes* on Shooting Stars—always happens the second week in August. When I was really little, Mama and Daddy would wake me up in the dead middle of the night (the best time to see the meteors) to watch some of it, but usually I just fell back asleep on Daddy's shoulder. Last year I was allowed to stay up for it, but I crashed out in bed waiting for it to start and *nobody* woke me back up. Grrr . . .

But *this year* . . . this year I not only get to stay up, I get to stay up WITH my best friends AT a sleepover ON the beach. Um, hello? Perfection-ish. And only "ish" because of the sand-in-the-sleeping-bag dilemma.

Because of the sea-turtle light restrictions plus how far away we are from any major cities (despite how my mom tries to spin it, I DO NOT count Wilmington as major), there's, like, zip zero light pollution at Sandpiper Beach. (For the record, light pollution sounds way less icky than other kinds of pollution.) That means we can see stars from one end of the horizon all the way to the other all year round, but it especially means we have ah-mazing views of the shooting stars. (And yes, Lauren would say they are meteors, which I actually know, but since they *look* like shooting stars, I'm so completely going with it.)

"Does anyone want any more 'Vi s'mores'?" Sadie asks. Our parents drew the line at a campfire, so Vi invented these cold s'mores–cookie bar things that are possibly, for real, even better than the actual thing.

"Hand 'em over," I order.

We chomp for a while, then take new stabs at getting into our bags. I finally accept that the sand is so totally gonna win this one.

We're quiet for a bit, listening to the waves crash in the dark and staring at the stars. I try not to blink while I wait (sorta, kinda) patiently for the first streak of light across the sky. I'm just starting to get all mellow in an I'm-just-a-tiny-fleck-in-the-giant-universe existentially way when Sadie says, "So, do y'all think we should go boy band or single act?"

All three of us turn our heads to her. "Huh?" I say at the same time as Lauren and Vi say, "What?"

"For the party next week," Sadie answers.

"Saaaaadie!" all three of us groan.

"Do you ever think of anything besides RSVP?" I ask.

"Yes!" Sadie answers, and she sounds a teeny-tiny bit defensive. Whoops. Hit a nerve. "But next week is our last full week off school, which means this is probably the last party of the summer, and I don't know about y'all, but I want to go out with a bang!"

We haven't talked at all about what happens to RSVP when summer ends. I think we're just assuming it'll end too. I pretty much am, because I know Lauren will never be on board with anything that interferes with her four-point-one-zillion grade point average, and Vi plays soccer, so I doubt we'd even have time for it anyway.

So last hurrah it is.

"Becs, I'm counting on you," Sadie says. "This is right up your alley."

"What, just because it's music-themed?"

Lauren laughs. "I think more because it's boy-band-crush-themed."

"I DO NOT crush on boy bands!" I screech. Then I mumble "anymore" under my breath.

Vi elbows me through her bag. "So are you saying you do *not* practice kissing on the poster of Trey Pestas that hangs on the back of your door?"

I elbow her back. Harder than she elbowed me. "Omigosh, seriously, y'all. I haven't kissed that poster in, like, six months. I barely even look at it anymore." No one needs to know that I had Daddy paint my bedroom walls the exact greenish blue as Trey's eyes to match the poster. My friends just don't appreciate a true musical artist when they see one.

I decide to switch the subject from Trey. "So, what are we thinking? Eight-year-old girls and a boy-band theme, right? Okay, so clearly all the girls need to dress like they're going to a concert. Rock-star chic. They'll obviously know what that means, right? Orrrrr, they could wear boy-band T-shirts. I could probably find one or two of my old One Direction nightshirts to donate to the cause."

Vi snickers. "One or two?"

I ignore her and keep talking. "Omigosh, and we for real have to get all of them sunglasses to wear—they can be the favors—and, like, autograph books for the fake band to sign and . . . man, it would be sooo awesome if we had a real fake band."

Lauren chimes in. "Actually, 'real fake' would be an oxymoron. That's when—"

"Lauren!" Vi yells, and her shout echoes out across the empty beach. "No vocabulary lessons. Let us enjoy our last ten days of freedom!"

Sadie is quieter when she says, "Well, the idea is a boy band and we do know a few boys we could ask. One in particular, who just happens to play an instrument . . ." I can't see her in the dark, but I know she's looking at me when she says, "I know you've been kind of weird about Ryan and that's why we didn't use him for Mr. Vernon's going-away party, but, Becs, you have to admit he'd be completely perfect for this. He has the hair and the accent and the guitar. The girls will totally eat him up."

She's so right, but *aaaaaaah*. I'm way too embarrassed around Ryan.

I mean, at least I learned my lesson and I'm not throwing myself at him anymore. No more bike crashes for me. The other day, he and Lance were in the line ahead of me, Sades, and Izzy at mini golf and when Lance asked us to join them, I was the one to say they should just go ahead so we could have girl time. I could tell Ryan was, like, ubershocked. His eyebrows were practically hidden in his bangs. But still. I bet he's gonna be happy to put an entire ocean between us when he goes back to Ireland.

"Please, Becs," Sadie asks, and I don't have to see her face to know her nose is doing that crinkly thing it does when she's begging for something.

"Fine," I sigh. "But then, I'm totally behind the scenes on this one. I'm so dead serious. And I am NOT going to ask him. Vi, that's all you. Because if I ask, he's never going to say yes."

"That's fine. Right, everyone?"

"Sure. I can ask him at volleyball," Vi says.

"Works for me," Lauren echoes.

"Totally behind the scenes," I repeat.

We're all quiet for a few seconds, peering at the stars some more. After a minute I can't keep silent anymore. "But we completely absolutely have to have a signature drink and name it after the birthday girl with, like, colored sugar dipped around the rims of the glasses. Rockstar parties always have that, I'm pretty positive."

Lauren and Vi giggle and Sadie reaches her hand over and tries to grab mine (I'm guessing), except she misses in the dark and ends up gripping my shoulder instead.

"Hey! *Look!*" Lauren's hand shoots out of her bag and points to a corner of the sky. We all swivel heads in time to catch the tiny trail of a meteor.

I quickly make a wish before it fizzles out.

"But, Daddy . . ."

"Don't 'But, Daddy' me, Rebecca Elise. You signed the Allowance Agreement, which stated your room had to be clean before cash was dispensed. Do you need me to produce the document?"

"No, but—"

"So if I was to walk home right now, I'd find a spotless room?"

"No, but—" I prop my elbows on the counter at the Visitor's Center and peer out through the sheets of rain at the statue of Merlin. I bet his dad never made him clean his seaweed house. Or wherever marlin live.

I'm working on a really perfect can't-resist argument when the little bells above the door clang and I whip my head up. I almost choke on my own spit when I see Ryan walking toward me with a cup of coffee in each hand.

"Daddy! Go hide!" I whisper-yell.

"We're in a glass box, Rebecca. Where would you like me to disappear to?"

"Anywhere," I moan. Luckily, Daddy pretends there's something he needs in the storage closet. As long as he doesn't come out with Polly Want a Cracker, we're good. Ryan reaches the counter.

"Halloo," he says, all softly, with that super-duper-delectable accent. I can't help it. Even after Sadie totally called me out on liking the idea of Ryan more than the actual person, my heart still flip-flops. It's the accent, I tell you.

I have to check behind my shoulder to make sure he's actually talking to *me*. Okay, so I really don't know what's going on here because once Sades and I had our talk, I kind of, sort of replayed all the Ryan moments from the summer in my head and basically realized that he pretty much was always trying to get away from me, which I was sooo totally stupid not to notice. So what the what is he doing here?

"Um, hi," I answer. *Hi, and could you please go away because I'm totally embarrassed around you, but also could you maybe not go away?*

Ryan holds up one of the cups of coffee. "For you. Peace offering."

Um . . . I'm kind of ashamed to admit that a few weeks ago I would have totally choked down that coffee if it meant I could have Ryan to myself the whole time I drank it, but I'm way more mature now.

"Thank you, but I don't drink coffee." I try not to wrinkle my nose when I say it, but *blech*!

Ryan looks relieved. "Oh good. Me either. I saw some of the other girls drinking it and, um, I thought maybe you did too."

"Nope. Mostly sweet tea."

Ryan smiles. "Yeah, sweet tea is one of the best things about this summer. We have plenty of tea in Ireland, believe me, but not like you have it here. I'll miss it when I go back next week."

I smile calmly (I think), but on the inside I'm screaming, *What. Are. You. Doing. Here?*

"Um, so do you want to go get some sweet tea, then?" Ryan asks.

Daddy coughs like he's choking on something. He's reappeared from the closet and is fake-busy rearranging the brochure display for fishing charters.

I decide to ignore him. "Um, sure, okay."

Ryan drapes his jacket over my head to keep the rain off as we run across the town square, and I have to stop myself from squeeing at how romantic that is. I mean, not romantic, of course, because he probably mostly finds me completely annoying, but still. So gentlemanly.

Once we order the tea (Omigosh—and he PAYS for mine! My mother always said you can tell the good ones by their manners and the way they treat their mamas. I bet she'd call Ryan a true Southern gentleman even if his South is all the way in Ireland), Ryan pulls out a chair for me at a table in the corner.

"So I bet you think this is kind of weird," he says.

Um, I basically would be less surprised if Lauren skipped school or Sadie forgot an item on her to-do list or Vi wore a dress. Oh wait, Vi did wear a dress. But still.

"Yeah, kind of," I mumble.

Ryan looks about as comfortable as I feel. Which is, like, not at all. He keeps dunking his straw up and down, up and down, in his sweet tea.

"So, the thing is, um, your company booked me for this gig. This band party, yeah?"

"Yeah," I say, nodding.

"And, uh, I'm supposed to be some rock star for these little girls, right?"

"Right." I nod again.

"But the problem is, I really can't play the guitar that well and, um, I was wonderingifyoucouldhelpme."

That last part came out like it was all one word. Oh. So that's what this is about. He needs my help.

He gives me a shy smile and I hide a sigh. It's not *Ryan's* fault I basically acted like a total idiot by practically throwing myself at him. He was pretty polite about it, considering I totally didn't take the hint. And he looks so helpless right now. How do I say no to him? Plus . . . accent! Accent all to myself for a little while before the summer ends. How do I say no to *that*?

"Yeah, sure. I can help. You seemed to have the basics down when I heard you play at the beach."

"The basics I'm good with, but I'm having some trouble with keeping the rhythm when I do my chord changes."

"Right. Some of that is just muscle memory, but it's also pretty common for beginners to try to tackle songs that are too advanced. Do you want to grab your guitar and meet me at Polka Dot Books in a half hour? There's an outdoor hangout spot in the back and I practice there a lot. It's protected from the rain and mostly private. Except for Cooper, the store's black Lab."

"Yeah? You're truly up for this?" Ryan asks.

"Sure. I have nothing going on this afternoon."

I fill Daddy in and race back to my house for my guitar. I have to wade through a pile of clothes on my floor to get to it. I have some time to kill since the bookstore is right next door, so I spend a couple minutes trying to make a dent in the mess, but I get bored pretty quickly. Guess it's an allowance-free week for Becca. I settle for a quick cuddle with Mr. Bobo. Despite my so-called bestie Vi calling my stuffed dog bald and one-eyed, he isn't even the tiniest bit sad-looking.

When I head over to the bookstore, Ryan is already there, strumming a song. He's not bad, but I spot a few bad habits right away. I fix his grip (Ack! Touching boy hands!!) and give him a few pointers, and then we jam a few songs. He picks up everything I teach him really fast.

"I wish I'd known you knew so much about guitar earlier this summer," he says.

I don't tell him it probably wouldn't have mattered earlier this summer, because I would have been too busy practicing my giggle on him to sit quietly next to him and play. But it's pretty nice now. I'm still totally aware there is a cute boy next to me—because, hello, let's be real—but I have to admit, I'm kind of having fun just hanging out like I would with my friends.

I smile. "Yeah, it's too bad."

"Right. I feel like it's my fault I formed an opinion of you early on. I'm really sorry I didn't get to know you better before now."

I just smile again. It's kind of awkward, though, and I don't really know what to say to that, so I'm pretty happy when he says he has to use the bathroom. I consider offering the one next door at my house, but Daddy would probably fuh-reak if I brought a boy home when no adults were there, so I don't mention it. While he heads off to the public restrooms down the street, I take the chance to work on my new song, the one Sadie inspired. It's coming along really well. Not well enough to show it to anyone, but I'm getting pretty excited about it.

"What's that one?" asks a voice from the doorway. I jump about ten feet in the air.

"Sorry," says Ryan. "I didn't mean to scare you."

"I thought you went to the bathroom!" I accuse.

"I did. Meg let me use the employee loo here."

Of course she did. Traitor. Meg always makes me run next door to use mine, but I guess even fifty-gazillion-something-year-olds are suckers for a good accent. I duck my head and start playing James Taylor's "Carolina in My Mind," but Ryan stops me with his hand on my guitar.

"Go back. Play the other one. It has a great hook. Whose song is that? Can you teach me the chords?"

I basically want to run up to my room and dive under the pile of clothes on the floor. Even though the rain is cooling things off today, my face is hotter than one of those freaking meteors we saw the other night.

"Um, it's nothing. Just something I'm working on."

I can't meet Ryan's eyes, but he's so quiet for so long that eventually I sneak a peek at him. He's staring at me with his mouth open. "You *wrote* that?"

"Um, yeah. It's not that good. I just—"

"Are you mad? It's *really* good. Does it have lyrics too?"

Hello, Earth? Could you please swallow me up now? Any time would be perfect. Like RIGHT now.

"Um, yeah. Sort of. I mean, I'm still working on them too."

Ryan doesn't let up. He pesters me and pesters me until I agree to teach him the song. At first I'm dead set against it, but I remind myself that (a) I opened up to Sadie and it wasn't like the world ended, and (b) Ryan's going to be an entire ocean away soon and I'll most likely never see him again.

So I show him.

Actually, he picks it up pretty quickly and comes up with an accompaniment that sounds really nice next to my lead guitar. After a few minutes of playing around with it, I kind of forget it's my song and just relax. Then I somehow get really, *really* relaxed (and also I keep reminding myself he's leaving town in a mere week) because I agree to run home and get my notebook with the lyrics and I actually *show them to him too*.

Eeep!!!!

But it's so totally cool because he doesn't laugh or tease me or anything. I think he's kind of even jealous of them or something. At least he says he is.

Of course, I draw the line at singing them. Huh-uh. No way.

But still. Major progress on Songwriting Becca front.

Also plus? Ryan's kind of a cool friend.

IT'S JILLY'S BIRTHDAY!

And you're invited to the biggest event to ever hit
Sandpiper Beach—a Five Alive Concert/Party!
When: Sunday, August 23, at two o'clock
Where: Sandpiper Park Pavilion, at the corner of
Bodington Drive & Cove Street
Dress: Rock-Star Chic!
You don't want to miss Jilly's surprise guests!
RSVP to Sadie Pleffer at (910) 555-0110 or
sadie@rsvpmail.com

16

Vi

GRAPE JELLY MEATBALLS

Ingredients:

5 lbs frozen meatballs

1 jar (32 oz) grape jelly

1 bottle (24 oz) chili sauce

Pour grape jelly and chili sauce into a Crock-Pot and whisk until it is smooth (there will still be some lumps from the jelly). Add frozen meatballs and stir until the meatballs are covered with the sauce. Put the lid on the Crock-Pot and cook on low for 6–7 hours (or high for 3–4 hours), stirring occasionally.

**Reminder: Don't tell anyone I use frozen meatballs instead of homemade!*

**Dad's favorite for the Super Bowl, the World Series, and pretty much any game on TV.*

Oh em gee, Lance, everyone knows JJ Jenkins always performs in a red shirt. It's his lucky color. Good thing I brought backup." Becca thrusts a bright red shirt at Lance.

Lauren and I stand there and blink at her.

"Well, everyone *does* know that . . . right?" Becca says.

"Sure, of course," Sadie says in a completely distracted voice. She's too busy messing with the sound system we rented from Darling's DJs to pay attention to Becca's uber–boy band knowledge.

"Um, no," Lauren adds.

"Yeah . . . no. Why don't we leave you to the band inspection, since you actually know this stuff?" I say. How she convinced each of these guys to dress up like one of the members of Five Alive is beyond me. Oh wait, I do know. We're paying them. Except she still couldn't convince *five* boys to dress up and dance to "I'm a Hot Potato," Five Alive's biggest song. So I guess it's more like Four Alive, which doesn't really have the same ring.

Becca waves us off as she shakes her head at Evan Miller's ball cap.

Lance comes out of the park bathrooms with the red basketball jersey on as I'm putting the food on a table under the covered picnic area. It's about ninety degrees out, and I'm doing my best not to drip sweat into the dishes.

"Nice shirt," I say with a smirk. It's kind of hilarious seeing Lance in this enormous oversized basketball jersey with JENKINS blazed across the back in huge white letters. And his hair is even funnier, all slicked back.

"Nice dress," he shoots back.

Seriously, why does everyone have to make a big deal about me wearing a dress? Okay, maybe it's not everyone—just Lance. My friends haven't said a word about me dressing differently (which is why I love them). Dad always does his goofy Dad-smile, but he knows better than to say anything. And I'm not about to explain to Lance that just because I like sports doesn't mean I always have to wear my comfy running shorts. In fact, this sundress is pretty comfortable too. I don't look up as I push the ham and cheese sandwiches front and center on the table.

"Sorry, Vi. I didn't mean that. I mean, it *is* a nice dress, but I didn't mean . . . well, you know."

His face is the color of a tomato when I look up and pass him the cord to the Crock-Pot full of meatballs.

"Plug that in, please." Good one, Vi. Totally calm and cool. Not at all completely freaked out by how weird Lance is acting.

"Um, sure." He uncoils the cord and plugs it into the nearest outlet.

I'm searching for the paper plates (seriously, it's like Lauren threw everything into the bags at random) when Lance makes this noise like he's just died and gone to heaven, as Meemaw would say.

"These are *so* good! Where did you get them?" He reaches for another meatball and I have to swat his hand away.

"Those are for the party," I tell him. "And they're made with grape jelly, that's why they're so good." I put the lid back on the Crock-Pot.

"Wait, did you make these?" He's looking at me like he has no clue who I am. "Seriously, Vi. That's the best thing I've ever eaten. I didn't know you could cook."

"Yeah, well." I can't really think of anything else to say. Plus it's weird talking to Lance about stuff that doesn't have to do with volleyball strategy or whether a tri-fin surfboard is better than a quad-fin. After Mr. Vernon's party, and the way everyone loved that crab dip, I wanted to try again just to see if it was a fluke—maybe the seniors were all a little senile.

Although Lance's reaction is telling me that possibly that's not the case. Which feels kind of good, if I'm being completely honest.

"Five Alive, rehearsal time. Now!" Becca shouts through cupped hands. "We need to run your dance number before the girls show up."

"Better go dance," I tell Lance. "Becca's pretty serious about this band stuff." I point with a serving spoon at Becca, who's got her hands on her hips as she waits for Lance and Ryan to join the other two guys.

By the time I've got the food ready, Lauren's arranged the Make Your Own Band T-Shirt table (complete with iron-ons of the Five Alive guys' faces and lots of glitter), Sadie's finally gotten the sound system set up, and Becca's run the boys through their dance three times and is handing them bottles of cold water so they won't pass out in the heat. The whole time, Izzy is darting around, taking pictures of it all. Sadie said she wanted to spend more time with her sister so she cooked up the idea to have Izzy play the role of paparazzi. We get everything ready just in time for the birthday girl, Jilly, to arrive with her parents and twenty of her closest eight-year-old friends.

Becca shoos the guys behind the bathrooms so the girls won't see them until the big reveal. Lauren, Sadie, and I hand out goody bags to all the girls as they come in, and Izzy snaps pictures of them. The girls ooh and aah over the bejeweled sunglasses and autograph books and the bracelets and rings that flash different colored lights (never mind that it's the middle of the afternoon and the sun is blinding, so you can barely see the lights).

"Are they dressed right?" Jilly's mom asks Sadie. "I wasn't entirely sure what 'rock-star chic' meant."

Lauren giggles and Sadie smiles at Jilly's mom. "They're perfect."

And they are. These kids have probably outdone Becca (who came in tight black leggings and the sparkliest shirt she owns). At least half of them have Five Alive T-shirts, they're practically drowning in costume jewelry, and Jilly's hair is teased up so high, it makes her almost as tall as me.

"Thanks again for doing this," Jilly's mom says. "I can't wait to see the band!"

"Well, let's get—" Sadie begins.

Becca's off and running onto the "stage," which is actually just the far side of the picnic area where we pushed the tables out of the way.

"Heeeey, party people!" Becca shouts through the microphone.

"—started," Sadie finishes.

The girls crowd around the stage area, Jilly right in front.

"I said, HEEEEY, PARTY PEOPLE!" Becca yells.

The girls clap.

Becca puts a hand on her hip and shakes her head, like the eight-year-olds are completely hopeless. "That's not the kind of welcome you give your most awesomely amazing BFF, Jilly Papadakis, is it? Especially not on her eighth birthday. And definitely not when she's got everyone's favorite band here to perform, just for all y'all!"

A few of the girls squeal, Jilly slaps her hands over her mouth and spins around to see her mom, and Mrs. Papadakis does a great job of acting super surprised.

"So let's make some NOISE!" Becca shouts so loudly, the people way down on the beach can probably hear her.

The girls scream and clap and jump up and down.

"Good call, putting her up there as the emcee," I say to Sadie.

"There's no way any of us could ever be that loud," Sadie replies with a grin.

"Or that enthusiastic over a bunch of guys from our class pretending to be some silly boy band," Lauren says.

"All right, then!" Becca says over the mic. "That's more like it! Now get ready for the most supremely amazing afternoon of your whole entire lives. Because here, just for you, Jilly, all the way from fabulous Toronto, Canada, ready to perform their number one song . . . FIVE ALIVE!!!!"

"And that's my cue," Sadie says just as the crowd of girls erupts into a synchronized shriek and Izzy's camera clicks in rapid succession. Lauren claps her hands over her ears as Sadie pushes her way toward the sound system.

Becca's jumping up and down "onstage," pumping her fist. So, of course, I can't help but pull out my Now-Sometimes-Vi lilac phone and snap a picture of her in midair just in case Izzy's protective of her own shots. Sadie starts some intro music, and Becca finally raises her hands to quiet the girls.

"Now some bad news. Leo Lumpkins has caught the duck flu, and can't join us today," Becca says.

Lauren laughs, and when I look at her, she whispers, "It's bird flu, not duck flu. It's this really horrible virus, and if the real Leo Lumpkins caught it, he'd be in pretty bad shape."

"Then I guess it's good we don't have a Leo Lumpkins." When we figured out we'd only have four guys, Becca suggested we leave out Leo. Apparently, he's the least popular. She actually called him Leo Lumpy, which seems kind of mean to me but she was like, "Please! Everyone calls him that."

Anyway, none of the girls look too disappointed that we don't have a Leo.

"So the only question is . . . ARE YOU READY?!" Becca shouts.

The girls scream and jump up and down.

"Here they are. FIVE ALIVE!"

Sadie turns the music up and Becca holds an arm out to her left.

And . . . nothing.

"Um, where are the guys?" Lauren asks.

Becca's onstage snapping her fingers all frantically (like the guys are actually going to hear that over the music).

"Be right back," I say to Lauren, and I race past the crowd toward the park bathrooms. Around the back of the concrete block building, I find Ryan, Lance, Evan, and this other guy, named Dominic, who's best known at school for bringing a veggie burger for lunch every single day. They're all hunched over Lance's phone.

I plant myself right in front of them.

Lance looks up. "Vi! You've gotta see this video of a dog jumping—"

I yank the phone from his hands. "Hello? There are a bunch of hyper eight-year-olds waiting for you! Move it! Or you'll have to answer to Becca."

That gets them going.

"Sorry," Lance says as he runs after the other guys toward the stage.

I join Sadie by the sound system as our Five Alive (Four Alive?) takes the stage. The girls either don't notice or don't care that they aren't the real Five Alive, because they're shouting and cheering so loudly that Sadie has to turn the music up when she starts "I'm a Hot Potato."

And I have to hand it to the guys. The dance isn't perfect, but they at least look like they rehearsed it. Ryan, who's playing the lead singer, even flashes some grins in between his lip-syncing that make the girls squeal even more.

As the song really gets going, I spot Becca singing along (to "I'm a hot potato, a potato in a tornado"),

Jilly's mom and a couple of other moms cheering and clapping along, and even Lauren bopping just a little to the beat in the back of the crowd.

"This is *perfect*," Sadie says as the song ends and the guys pose onstage.

The girls scream and shout for more. Except the guys only rehearsed one song, so that's not going to happen. But it doesn't seem to matter, because Ryan gives the crowd a wink, and then he's mobbed—like swarming-bees mobbed—by shrieking eight-year-olds, with Izzy right in the middle, capturing it all with her camera.

"Omigod! Get them out of there! Where are the bodyguards? Hey, girls, back off the talent!" Becca's trying to part the sea of girls to get to Ryan and the others.

I look at Sadie and we both burst out laughing.

"Maybe we should help her," I say between giggles.

"Probably," Sadie says. But before we can take a step, Becca emerges from the pack of girls, arms out to each side, protecting the guys as they run off toward the bathrooms.

"Whew," she says when the moms finally step in and guide the girls toward Lauren and the Make Your Own Band T-Shirt table.

"Um . . ." I point to her hair, which was in this nice slicked-back ponytail and is now in a not-so-nice sticking-straight-up mess.

Becca pats her head and makes a face. "Be right back."

The party's going really well. The T-shirts are a hit, the girls eat pretty much all the food and cake (and I'm kind of proud to say that my meatballs went first), they drink gallons of pink Jilly-ade, Jilly's opened all her presents, and Sadie's kept the Five Alive music pumping through the stereo. Becca brings the guys back so the girls can get their autographs.

Sadie's just about to restart the Five Alive album when Jilly taps her on the shoulder.

"Hey, do you have any other music?" Jilly asks.

"I'm sorry, all we brought was Five Alive," Sadie says. "I thought you and your friends loved the band?"

I'd say they more than loved the band, considering the way they lined up for the guys' autographs and giggled every time Ryan or Lance said a word to them.

"We *adore* Five Alive," Jilly says. "But all their songs are about love and kissing and stuff." She makes a face like this is just totally gross.

"So, what do you want to hear?" I ask her.

"I don't know. A song about friends, maybe?"

"I'll scroll through my phone and see if I can find anything," Sadie says. She flicks on her phone, and then turns it off. "Wait. I just had the *best* idea." She runs off toward Becca.

Jilly looks at me, and I shrug.

Sadie's talking to Becca, and Becca's shaking her head. What in the world? Sadie grabs Becca's hand and drags her over to me and Lauren.

"Okay, so here's the deal," Sadie says. "Becca—"

"Shh! It's a secret." Becca's eyes are huge and she looks like she wants to clamp a hand over Sadie's mouth.

"What's going on?" Lauren asks.

"Becs, these are your best friends. No one's going to laugh at you. Just tell them, already!" Sadie says as she gathers her hair up in a ponytail.

Becca eyes the ponytail—Sadie's getting-down-to-business one—which pretty much means Sadie's not going to give up until Becca spills the beans.

She gives a huge sigh and then mumbles, "Iwrisngs."

"What?" I ask.

Becca's face matches her hair by now. "I. Write. Songs."

None of us says anything for a couple of seconds.

"Ugh, why did you make me tell?" Becca asks Sadie. "They think it's stupid."

Not exactly. Lauren has this look on her face like she couldn't be more impressed.

I shake my head. "It's not stupid! It's really cool, actually. But, um, Sades, what does this have to do with Jilly and the playlist for the party?"

"Becca told me—" Sadie starts, but Becca takes over.

"Oh my gosh, if everyone has to know everything, then fine. Sadie gave me this great idea to write a song about friendship, and so . . . I did. And then I kinda, mighta shown . . ." Becca trails off.

"Shown . . . ?" Lauren prompts.

"Ryan, okay? I showed Ryan." I've never seen Becca look more embarrassed. Ever. I didn't think she was actually capable of being embarrassed. It's So Not Becca.

But then again, maybe a lot of us are more than what we show the world.

"You did?" Lauren squeals. I also did not know Lauren could squeal.

"And he *loved* it," Sadie adds, looking all proud of

Becca. "So . . . don't y'all think it'd be great if Becca and Ryan performed the song here?"

"Yes!" Lauren and I say together.

"No. No way. Nuh-uh," Becca says.

Ryan appears behind Becca. "Wait, are you talking about Becca's song? I'll sing it with you," he says to Becca.

"No, I don't—"

"No excuses! Come on, let's get our guitars. Which guy was pretending to play yours in the show?"

Becca's eyes are wide as she murmurs, "Lance, but . . ."

Ryan doesn't wait for her to say any more. Looking so excited to perform, he runs off to grab both instruments.

"You can thank us later," Sadie says as she pushes Becca toward where Ryan is headed onto the stage. "Izzy, heads up. You're gonna want your camera ready for this!" she calls to her sister.

Becca stumbles forward. "I'm never talking to you again. Any of you." But when Ryan holds out her guitar, she sighs and goes to join him.

Sadie runs after her and grabs the mic. "Hey, everyone, we have a special treat for you. This is the world premiere of, um . . . the, uh, Becca and Ryan Experiment."

Behind her Becca makes a face, and Ryan flushes so much you'd think someone just outed that he still plays with his Thomas the Tank Engine trains or something.

The girls crowd around. Lauren and I push our way over to Sadie after she leaves the stage to Becca and Ryan.

Sadie's beaming as Becca strums her guitar. The song is slow and mellow. It's nothing like the Five Alive pop songs, but none of the partygoers seem to mind. They're wholly focused on the stage. I flick on my phone and hold it up to capture the whole thing. Ryan joins in with his guitar, and then Becca starts singing, really quietly:

"You can blow out the candles on
     your cake,
  Close your eyes and make a wish.
  You can meet for your reunion
     once a year,
  Pass around your favorite dish."

"I didn't know Becca could sing or write songs," Lauren says. "And I thought she was too embarrassed to even talk to Ryan, never mind play music with him.

Although they did kind of have a moment at Illumination Night."

I can't say anything. I'm just standing there, my phone in the air, staring at my boy-crazy, kind-of-over-the-top friend, carefully singing this song that she wrote.

Ryan picks up the next verse:

"You can tick off days until you
   reach it,
Make your lists and check them
   twice.
You can send out invitations,
Buy the costumes and the ice."

"I didn't know *Ryan* could sing," Sadie says.

Invitations. Costumes. Ice. "Is this about parties?" I ask. But no one has an answer.

Becca sings,

"But I'll be celebrating
All the ordinary Tuesdays,
I'll be holding out for
Laughs along the shore,

We'll be singing
La la la la la la la la,
'Cause life is so much more
Just shared among us four."

"Wait . . ." Lauren turns toward Sadie.

At the same time I put it together. "Becca wrote this about us, didn't she?"

Sadie's smiling. "I think she totally did. It's kind of amazing, isn't it?"

"It's about us," Lauren repeats softly.

Ryan takes up the next verse.

"You can have your parties and
   your presents,
I don't need no occasion to
   commend,
No holidays, no anniversaries,
Just a random day to be with
   friends.
And I'll be celebrating
All the ordinary Tuesdays,
Holding out for

> All the laughs along the shore.
> We'll be singing
> La la la la la la la la,
> 'Cause life is so much more
> Just shared among us four."

The girls around the stage are swaying in time to the music, but I can't take my eyes off Becca. She wrote a song. About us. My heart feels so full it could burst. I grab Lauren's hand, and she takes Sadie's, as Becca and Ryan sing together,

> "If I didn't have you to bump
>   through life with,
> It wouldn't be any fun at all.
> And sometimes the thing I take
>   for granted,
> Is having you there whenever
>   I call.
> And we'll be singing:
> La la la la la la la la,
> 'Cause life is so much more
> Just shared among us four."

Becca gives her guitar one last strum, and she finally meets our eyes. I clap and cheer, and everyone else joins in. She smiles, and both she and Ryan take a bow. Someone sniffles next to me. I turn just in time to see Lauren swipe at her eyes.

"Are you crying?" I ask her.

"No!" But she won't look at me. I grin at Sadie over Lauren's head, and when Becca appears in front of us, we all grab her in one huge hug.

"Why didn't you ever say anything before this?" I give her a fake punch on the arm.

"I don't know. I guess I was just searching for the right song," she says. "So . . . you liked it?"

"Of *course* we liked it! We loved it," Sadie says.

"Becca!" Lauren grabs her into another bear hug.

"Are you crying?" Becca asks through a faceful of Lauren's hair.

"No. Maybe. Who cares? You're the best best friends ever! I can't believe I almost missed out on all of this." Lauren rubs at her eyes again. "Ugh! Let's stop with this and dance! Sadie, where's that Living Five music?"

Becca bursts out in laughter while Sadie motions to Ryan to turn on the music. "I'm a Hot Potato" echoes through the speakers. Lauren grabs our hands and we dance, right alongside half the eight-year-old population of Sandpiper Beach.

We're helping Jilly's mom load the gifts into her car when Sadie looks across the parking lot and sighs.

"Sades, I'm so sorry your mom was a no-show again. You okay?" I ask her.

Sadie shrugs. "Actually . . . I didn't even mention it to her this time."

Whoa. "How come?"

Another shrug. "I don't know. All summer part of every party has been spent watching the door for my mom or being upset when she's texted me saying she couldn't make it. I didn't want that hanging over today. RSVP might have started out as a way to prove myself to my mom, but it means something different to me now, you know?"

I balance the presents on my right arm and wrap my left around Sadie's shoulders. "If she'd been here, you could've taught *her* a thing or two about party planning."

"Yeah," Becca chimes in. "This was one seriously ah-mazing party."

"We probably made Jilly the most popular almost-third-grader in the history of Sandpiper Beach," Lauren adds.

"And now we have our own theme song. Thanks to Becca," I say.

Sadie smiles. "I have the best friends ever. And, you know, my mom doesn't have a theme song for her business, so . . ."

"Reason number 657 that RSVP is better," Lauren says.

"Hey, um, Vi?" I turn around to see Lance, wearing his JJ Jenkins clothes and silly slicked-back hair.

The presents in my arms shift a little, and I have to tighten my grip around them.

"Here." Lance holds out his hands. "Let me take those."

"That's okay. I'm fine."

Becca jabs me with her elbow full of extra goody bags. "Let him," she whispers, sort of.

"Um. Okay. I guess."

Lance takes the boxes and toys. He walks with us the rest of the way to Jilly's mom's car. And doesn't say anything.

We load everything inside, and then he smiles at me, all awkward-like.

"So, see ya at school this week?" he asks.

"I'll be there." Because I can't *not* be there.

"Okay. Great." He tries to shove his hands in his pockets, but the giant basketball jersey is in the way. "So, um, yeah."

"Yup," I say.

"All right. Bye." And he walks off toward home.

Sadie bursts into laughter while Becca shakes her head.

"Vi, you need some coaching in making actual conversation," Lauren says.

"Forget conversation. She needs flirting lessons," Becca says.

"No and no." I'm so embarrassed, I could melt right into the boiling pavement under our feet.

"Girls!" Jilly's mom comes running up from the picnic area. "Thank you SO much for this party. You were great. And that song about friendship was genius." She pulls some bills from her wallet and hands them to Sadie. "This is what I owe you, plus a little more. Jilly will be talking about this party for the next year. Speaking of next year, can I book you now for her ninth birthday party?"

We look at each other. None of us has brought up what's going to happen with RSVP once school starts this week.

"Can we let you know?" Sadie asks.

After we load up the sound system and empty food containers into Becca's mom's SUV, we count and split up the money, setting aside enough to pay the guys. Adding it to what I already have, it's more than enough to buy Vi's Most Wanted. No matter what I think about his new job, Dad completely deserves something good. And while I guess he thinks being the janitor is something good, new kayaks are way better and definitely less embarrassing.

"I feel like we should celebrate," Lauren says.

"Don't you need to study?" Sadie asks.

Lauren waves a hand. "I'm good. We've been so busy planning parties for everyone else, it's our turn to have one. To celebrate the end of summer. Let's get snacks and meet at the *Purple People Eater* in one hour." She swipes at her forehead. "I'll bring a fan."

That is So Not Lauren, but none of us are going to argue with her.

Sadie

17

TODAY'S TO-DO LIST:
☐ dissolve RSVP

The air is sticky as ever and the setting sun still bakes the wooden planks of the dock as I drag my wagon along it. There's nothing in the weather that screams, "End of summer!" but I feel it anyway.

Tomorrow Bubby and Lauren's mom are taking us all back-to-school shopping and I'll be trying on sweaters and pants and coats (and trying to steer clear of Bubby's fashion suggestions). Yesterday my new backpack came in the mail. School starts in four days and summer is over.

Just like that.

The wagon wheel catches in the space between two

planks and I have to tug it free. I make my way to the very last slip, where the *Purple People Eater* bobs with the waves.

"I could use a hand!" I call to whoever's inside. Lauren pokes her head out.

"Hand with what?"

"ICE!" I proclaim triumphantly. "I thought the occasion called for actual *cold* beverages."

Lauren grins and steps out onto the deck of the *PPE*. "Vi, get ready. I'm tossing this in to you."

We form a bucket brigade and hoist the giant bag of ice into the boat. Next up I pass over pink lemonade mix and a jar of crushed-up rock candy and climb down into the boat's cabin. "Who says only movie stars can have signature drinks? I thought we deserved our own to toast the summer and the end of RSVP."

Lauren must've nabbed the battery-operated fan from the marina's office, because there's actually a breeze inside the cabin. Vi's trying to arrange a plate of her homemade pita chips but Lauren keeps sneaking them off the plate and into her mouth as fast as Vi puts them out. She swats Lauren's hand away and glances at me.

"So, are we really calling it quits?" Vi asks. "I mean, I assumed, with school starting and everything, but we never actually said it, so . . ."

There's a loud thud outside and Lauren uses the railings on either side of the stairs to pull herself up. She pokes her head out, then drops back in. "Becca's bike. It's like she's allergic to her kickstand."

Becca's shadow appears in the hatch and then she does. "Hey, gorgeous people." She heads down the stairs, perches her butt on the second step, and grins at us. "What'd I miss?"

"Nothing yet. We were just getting ready to toast the end of a perfect summer," Vi says.

"And a perfect company," I add, dumping lemonade mix into four glasses and stirring, while trying not to knock off any of the rock candy I've coated the rims with. I probably should have done the lemonade in a pitcher first, since I'm not having too much luck with it.

"Toasting RSVP or saying good-bye to it?" Becca asks.

"Saying good-bye, I guess."

We all look around at each other, but no one speaks.

Finally Vi says, "Which is probably just as well. I mean, I have soccer starting soon and then I'm going to go pick up the kayaks. I can't wait to see my dad's face! But, yeah, I guess it makes sense to be done. . . ."

She sort of trails off and Lauren takes a deep breath. "Yeah. My after-school tutoring starts up in two weeks and—"

"Seriously, y'all!" Becca looks the same way she did when she was yelling at Jilly's friends to make more noise for Five Alive. "How can we be done just like that? RSVP was the best part of the summer. Remember Bubby's jeggings and me on the plantation house floor covered in fake blood and—"

"The moss dress!" Lauren giggles.

Vi rolls her eyes and says, "Don't remind me. I think I still have a rash from that."

"Becca's song," I add, and all the girls turn to Becca, who covers her eyes with her hand. It's so far from a typical gesture from her that I have to hold in a laugh.

"Best song ever," Lauren says. "Really."

Vi holds up her phone and jiggles it back and forth. "I captured it all for easy playback whenever we need a pick-me-up."

"I need a pick-me-up right now," Becca says with a

sigh. "No more summer, no more parties. Nothing but boring seventh grade to look forward to."

I know what she means. Even though I'm kind of weird and tend to get really excited about new school years (all those perfectly perfect blank organizers and new pens and Post-it notes and a fresh, clean wipe board for my locker that doesn't have remnants of old marker smudges), I'll miss this summer. Everyone gets so busy with their own stuff once school starts.

Speaking of busy with her own stuff, as much fun as RSVP was, despite what I told Lauren earlier about RSVP meaning something different to me now—and it does!—it still didn't ever manage to do the one thing it was supposed to. It didn't show my mom how great I am at party planning. She never even made it to a single party.

I don't really know if I would even want her to offer me my job back, because why should I have to throw myself at her just to get her to spend some time with me? Shouldn't she want to all on her own?

So, yeah, I guess RSVP didn't solve anything with my mom the way it was supposed to. But I'm still glad we did it. So, so glad. And I'm completely bummed to dissolve it even if it does make the most sense.

"We could always do it again next summer," Lauren says. "We do have one job offer on the table already, from Jilly's mom."

"Next summer is, like, for*ever* away." Becca sounds glum and I have to say, it really *does* sound far away. We all take tiny sips of our drinks, but the atmosphere is anything but celebration-like.

"Look, maybe if everyone feels this sad about it, we could find a way to—"

"If I didn't have you to bump through life with . . ."

Becca's eyes get all wide. "You made my song your RINGTONE?!" she accuses me.

I grab for my purse. "Well, yeah. I told you I loved it."

"I know, but . . ." Becca's eyes look like she might be getting teary. Awww. I reach over and squeeze her leg.

"La la la la la . . ."

"Is someone gonna answer that?" Vi asks, pointing at the phone in my hand.

Oh. Whoops.

"Hello?"

The person on the other end clears her throat. "Is this RSVP?"

"Um . . . yes. Yes, this is RSVP. Sadie speaking."

I raise my eyebrows at the other girls and quickly hit the speakerphone button on my cell because I know Vi was just about to hassle me to do it anyway.

I put the phone in the center of our circle and say, "How may we help you?"

"My name is Alexandra Worthington. I've been hearing your company's name all over town. First from a woman in my yoga class, raving about her daughter's birthday party. Then from a man at my country club, talking about a shindig he attended with his dad at the senior center. It got me thinking. The last straw came when a woman I've been working with couldn't stop raving about the work you do. The thing is, I think she might have talked herself out of a job. Because the more she raved about you, the more I started thinking, 'Well, if they're so good, maybe I should be using them instead of you, lady.' So my question is this: Can you women handle big events?"

Women? That's kind of a stretch, but this lady sounds pretty fancypants. Maybe that's just how she talks to everyone.

"Um . . ." I look around at the girls. Becca catches my eye and starts nodding her head like crazy. I look at Vi, who shrugs. Lauren next. She looks hesitant, but curious. *Maybe?* she mouths. We all grin. Could be RSVP isn't as dead as we thought.

"Of course. No event is too big or too small. What type of event did you have in mind?"

"A wedding. My wedding, to be specific."

My spine gets this little prickle right in the base and it works its way up my back. "Where did you say you heard about us?"

"From my wedding coordinator. She couldn't stop going on about how she'd been keeping tabs on RSVP's parties all summer and how excited she was about the work you were doing. She said if she wasn't careful you'd put her out of business someday. Like I said, it made me curious. I insist on the very best for my wedding, and if Lorelei Pleffer thinks you're it, I want you."

Lorelei Pleffer? Lorelei Pleffer, my *mom*?

Our grins turn to wide-eyed stares and my stomach churns right alongside my thoughts. My mom's been keeping tabs on my parties? Why wouldn't she have told me that? She thinks we're good enough to put her out of business someday? Which, obviously, is silly because this was (is still?) just a summer company, but the fact that she would even say something like that . . .

And now her bride wants to jump ship from her and hire us instead?

We'd be basically *stealing* a client from my own mother. Could I do that? I know I'm super mad and hurt about the way everything's gone down this summer and all, but that seems pretty extreme. Besides, now that I know she's been saying all this nice stuff about RSVP, am I even that mad? More important, how mad would *she* be? Would she ever forgive me?

Then again, I wanted Mom's attention, and oh boy, would this get it. But do I dare?

"Hello? Are you still there? I expect an answer to my question. This isn't the best way to impress me right out of the gate. Did our connection drop? *Hello?*"

Becca leans over and speaks directly into the phone. "We're still here, and nothing would thrill us more than to coordinate your wedding. We're your girls, Miss Worthington!"

Oh. No. She. Didn't. Just. Do. That.

My jaw drops as Becca looks at me and shrugs.

Oh my gosh, she did.

ACKNOWLEDGMENTS

All the parties ever should be held in honor of:

Amy Cloud, for being a big-city girl who's kept all her small-town sweetness, for sometimes using "totes" in conversation without a hint of irony (because what's more lovable than that?), and for once braving a screaming 5 Seconds of Summer crowd in the name of research. Also for being a whip-smart editor who knew just how and where to tease more emotion out of this story (and for turning Becca from a Samantha into a Charlotte.)

The entire Aladdin team, who works tirelessly behind the scenes.

Holly Root, agent extraordinaire, whose last name is oh-so-appropriate, because I always feel she's doing just that for both me and my stories (and who will totally roll her eyes and smile at the cheesiness of that statement!).

Gail Nall, for making me snort coffee as I read her chapters and for forcing me to up my game to be sure she did the same when reading mine. We may not be so great at hailing taxis in Manhattan, but we sure do work seamlessly together on this book-writing stuff, and I couldn't be more grateful for that! (Google Docs probably gets a share of credit here too!)

Marieke Nijkamp, for careful reads and "just because" love letters—she is the stuff critique-partner dreams are made of.

I order confetti cannons fired in honor of:

Dee Romito, for general awesomeness. There's a reason the coolest house in this book bears her name.

Jean Lyon, for keeping me sane and reminding me: "poster shop!"

Jenny Lundquist, for early input and cheerleading.

Grace Mann, for composing the music for and singing Becca's song far better than could ever be imagined. (You can hear it for yourselves at jenmalonewrites.com and gailnall.com.) No doubt someday people will be asking, "Wow, how on earth did you score *Grace Mann* to sing for you?"

Darren Macke, Lauren Magaziner, and Nathalie Alexander for weighing in on guitar lingo. I'm incredibly jealous of you all, and please invite me to your next beach bonfires.

Geraldine Leahy, for double-checking Ryan's "Irish-isms."

And extra-special balloon bouquets for:

My family. Jack and Ben for reading and championing Mom's books, even when they get more "girly," not less so. Caroline, for constant inspiration and breaktaking cuddles. And for my sweet husband, John, who pretends not to be a big reader but always knows exactly how to read *me*.

Ocean Park, Maine. Most would never believe that Sandpiper Beach, with its kazoo-banded Fourth of July parade and old-fashioned soda fountain, is a real place, but that's just because they've never been to Ocean Park, whose own Illumination Night is a sight to behold. I'm proud five generations of my family have shared in its summer magic and I hope my own "penny to the mermaid statue" wishes continue to come true.

Last, for all the girls and women from childhood to now whose friendship allowed me to write about these besties from the heart, and for all the girls reading who see themselves in Becca or Sadie or Vi or Lauren. Girls rock!

—J. M.

First of all, to you, the reader of this book—thank you! I'm so happy you picked this book to read, and Jen and I hope you find a little of yourself in the RSVP girls. Feel free to drop me a note at gailnall.com—I'd love to hear from you!

To Amy Cloud, who totes mcgoats gets Bubby, and who loves Sadie, Vi, Becca, and Lauren as much as we do. You helped make the girls into the fun, well-rounded characters they are now, and we'd be lost without you! We owe you your very own Wanda and bucketloads of cupcakes. To everyone at Aladdin who showed such enthusiasm for *You're Invited*, and who touched this book in any way—thank you!

To Julia A. Weber, the best agent a girl could ask for. And who is probably the only person I know who could rock the Dread Pirate costume for Halloween and looked insanely good doing so.

To Dee Romito, Stefanie Wass, Jenny Lundquist, and Marieke Nijkamp, who read various pieces and parts of *You're Invited*. Thank you for your suggestions, love notes, and encouragement! A million thanks to Grace Mann for RSVP's theme song! Thanks also to the MG Beta Readers and the LL&N critique group, for coming along on this crazy writing ride with me. And more thanks to Gretchen Kelley, Sara O'Bryan Thompson, my agency sisters, my writer friends in SCBWI Midsouth, and everyone at St. John Center, simply for being there.

To Jen Malone—writing with you is a hundred times more fun than writing alone! Thanks for letting me text you lyrics to early nineties classics and for pushing me to be a better writer. I can't think of anyone else with whom I'd rather share a $250/night, sardine-can, book-stuffed NYC hotel room.

To my family—Mom and Joel, who have salt water running through their veins; Dad, who braved the freezing Plum Island waters with me when I was a kid; Cheryl, who can still boogie-board with the best; and Linda, Mike and Joann, and Lisa and David. And to Eva, who is just discovering the joy of the beach.

Finally, to the towns of Oak Island and Southport, North Carolina, upon which much of Sandpiper Beach is very loosely based. It doesn't come much better than a Cape Fear sunset, a fascinating pirate-y history, some perfectly shaped scallop shells, and an uncrowded beach.

—G. N.

TURN THE PAGE FOR A PEEK AT WHAT'S
IN STORE FOR SADIE, BECCA, LAUREN,
AND VI IN *YOU'RE INVITED TOO.*

Sadie

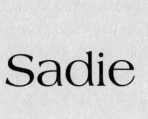

TODAY'S TO-DO LIST
- ☐ meet with bride
- ☐ back-to-school shopping with Bubby and the girls
- ☐ break Mom's heart

*S*o this *thing* just happened.

Well, not "just" just, but "just" as in yesterday. And ever since then I've been walking around with an iron anchor in my belly that jumps every so often, because this *thing* that happened is either going to be the best thing ever . . . or the worst thing ever.

Or maybe even both.

It's also the reason I'm out of bed at six a.m. on the third-to-last day of summer. All the girls in our family—

me, Mom, and my little sister, Izzy—are rise-and-shine, early-bird-gets-the-worm people, but six o'clock in the summer is kind of a stretch. If Dad were still alive, he'd have seventeen pillows piled on top of his head right now and nothing short of waving a can of coffee beans under his nose would wake him up.

Mom doesn't hear me coming down the stairs, so I have a minute to study her. Her hands circle a mug of tea and a few strands fall out of a messy ponytail. She doesn't look like she's been up too long either. She also doesn't look like she slept that well.

My stomach takes another dive, like the pelicans circling the cove outside our window for fishy breakfasts. Am I the reason she was up all night? Not that she would know I was involved yet, but . . .

I tiptoe over to my purse on the wooden bench by the back door and rifle through it for my phone. Mom still doesn't notice me.

Okay, so here's the thing. All last year I helped my mom with her wedding-planning business and it was Awesome-with-a-capital-A because Mom's crazy busy, and working with her meant we got to hang out together. I *thought* she needed me because I was her best helper. But then I made a teeny-tiny bridesmaid-overboard/

seagull-pooping/photographer-puking mistake at this *Little Mermaid*–themed wedding she coordinated and—poof—I got fired.

FIRED!

By my own mother.

But *then* my three best friends and I cooked up this plan where we would organize a party ourselves to get my mom to realize how totally fantastic I am at party throwing and hire me back. Except that didn't happen. The party happened—lots of parties, actually, because after the first one went so well we just kept going with more and more—but Mom never made it to any of them and she never got to see me in action at all.

Mostly it wasn't her fault, but still.

I flip through my texts, looking to see if there are any changes to our morning meeting spot. Despite my mood, I can't help smiling at a selfie my best friend Becca sent late last night. She's wearing a tiara. If I know Becca, she probably slept in the thing.

Because of Becca—and my other best friends, Lauren and Vi—it didn't even matter that much that Mom hadn't changed her mind about hiring me back, because our little party-planning company, RSVP, got so busy and I was having so much fun with my friends that I ended up having the Best Summer Ever and everything felt really okay. Better than okay.

And then yesterday happened.

I drop my phone back in my bag and turn, accidentally making the floorboard creak. Mom's head snaps up.

"Geez, Sades, you scared me half to death. What are you doing creeping around? More importantly, what are you doing *up*?"

I cross the room and duck my head into the refrigerator so she can't see my face. I don't usually—scratch that, I don't *ever*—lie to my mom.

"Oh, um, well . . . I'm just really excited for shopping today." Not technically a lie. Going into the city is exciting (okay, so it's just Wilmington, North Carolina, and not, like, New York City, but when you live somewhere as small as Sandpiper Beach, anywhere that has dividing lines painted on the roads and four-way traffic lights passes for big time.)

"Oh, right," Mom says. "Back-to-school shopping. Hang on, let me grab my credit card. You remember the limit we talked about, right? Things are tight this month, okay? And Lauren's mom and Bubby will be there if the store gives you any hassle over using this."

She rummages in her purse and hands me the piece

of plastic. I swallow down my guilt as I take it. I feel extra bad going on a shopping spree(ish) just before she finds out I'm a total backstabber. I really need to get out of here.

I gulp down some orange juice and grab a banana for the road. "I'm going over to Becca's to help her sort her closet by color so she can spot any underrepresented shades before we hit the shops."

This is actually true. It's just that it's happening later this morning, not right this second.

"Okay, sweets. Have fun!"

I'm halfway out the door when Mom calls me back. Uh-oh. Is she onto me?

"Hey, I just wanted to remind you, whatever you do, do *not* take Lauren's Bubby's advice on skirt length. If it's not hitting mid-thigh when you sit, it doesn't come home with you! Got it?"

I nod and spin, making a run for the door and my bike.

The girls and I are meeting Alexandra Worthington at Salty Stewart's Café in the main square. Most of the businesses in Sandpiper Beach are clustered around the center, by the big statue of Merlin the Marlin.

Merlin's this giant brass fish that's supposed to be a life-size representation of the biggest Atlantic marlin ever recorded, caught in 1942 by a descendent of our town's founder, Jebediah Bodington. If you live here, it's practically the law to know this stuff, but I get constant reminders every time I sneak in on the walking tours Becca has to give all the time because her mom and dad run the Visitor's Center. Becca gets most of *her* information from Lauren, our resident smarty-pants.

I'm the first one to Stewie's (as us locals call it), so I grab the long table and wave to Lance. He's going into seventh grade with us and I have a sneaky feeling he's crushing on Vi, but she's way too blind to see it. His grandfather (Stewie himself) owns the place, his mom and dad run it, and sometimes (like today) Lance buses tables.

"Water?" he calls over as he wipes down a seat.

"Five, please," I answer.

Becca is next through the door, which makes sense since she lives closest.

"This humidity is inhumane. It took me for-*ev*-er to straighten this. I swear, I think the stars were still out when I started." Becca runs a hand through her shoulder-length red hair and grimaces.

Lauren and Vi push through the door one right after the other and grab chairs. "Who knew there was life on the island at o-dark-thirty?" Vi asks.

Lauren looks at her funny. "Vi, this island had its start as a fishing village. In 1769, when Jebediah Bodington incorporated the town, it's likely that everyone was up at five a.m. trawling the Intercoastal for shrimp."

"Thanks for the history lesson, Lo," Vi says, sticking out her tongue and then ducking her head when she catches sight of Lance. "Who's ordering the liver?"

It's kind of a long-running joke among us because Stewie's has liver and chicken steak on the breakfast menu, right next to pancakes and omelets.

"French toast for me," I say. "But don't you think it would be more polite to wait for Alexandra Worthington?"

"Alexaaaaaandra Worthingtoooooooon," Becca says, drawing out the name and using a slight British accent. "It sounds so fancy. What do you think she looks like? My bet is she's a total glamourpuss."

The door tinkles and a woman teeters in on seventeen-inch heels (approximately), wearing a hat I've only seen people in the stands at the Kentucky Derby wear. It's purple straw and so wide it brushes the sides of the door. She's paired it all with a tiny tube top that shows off a giant tattoo of some kind of bird covering her entire left shoulder and a pair of too-tight black capri pants. Whoa. I don't really know if "glamourpuss" is the right term. More like a weird cross between royalty and . . . I don't really know what.

"Do you think that's her?" Vi whispers.

Becca cranes her head around. "Ooooooh yeah."

"Do. we go over?" Lauren asks.

"I think it would be more professional if she came to us, right? Just look busy. And important." Becca shoves a menu at each of us, while throwing her head back and letting out a fake laugh that can only be described as "tinkling."

I peek over my menu to watch Alexandra Worthington's eyes sweep right over our table and then turn away to peer down at her watch with a frown. She's still hovering just inside the doorway.

"I don't think it's working, guys. I'm gonna go get her." I push my chair back and make my way to the front. "Excuse me, by any chance are you Alexandra Worthington?"

She looks at me and one eyebrow lifts (I'm so in awe of people who can do that.) "I am. I'm sorry. I can't really chat, though. I'm supposed to be meeting someone, or rather, a group of someones. Though they're late, which is inexcusable, really." She begins to pick at a thread on her tube top.

"Oh, no, actually, we're all here. See?" I gesture to our table where Becca, Lauren, and Vi give little waves. Lauren's is a regular one, Vi's is more of a tomboy kind of hand flick, and Becca's cupped fingers and back-and-forth motion make her look like Miss America on a parade float. I can't help grinning at all three of them.

"Beg your pardon? I'm afraid there's been a mis-understanding. I'm meeting four women who run a wedding-planning business," Alexandra Worthington says.

"Party-planning, really," I say. "You'll be our first wedding."

Oh yeah. The thing that happened yesterday? It's this: Becca, Lauren, Vi, and I were meeting at the *Purple People Eater*, which is what we call the abandoned yacht that we turned into our clubhouse. The whole point of our meeting was to dissolve our little summer company and say good-bye to the Best Summer Ever. But then, right as we were toasting RSVP with glasses of lemonade, the phone rang and it was Alexandra Worthington, wanting to know if she could book us to plan her wedding.

Up till now, we've mostly been doing birthday parties for kids plus a few parties at the senior center (where Lauren's sorta-crazy grandmother Bubby lives), which were basically matchmaking ventures to get Bubby together with the elderly guy she was crushing on. They were great and we rocked them, but they weren't anything on the level of a wedding.

But when Alexandra Worthington called, she said she'd been hearing our name all over town. I guess people really liked the parties we planned and, well, Sandpiper Beach is really tiny and the rule of living somewhere really tiny is that you have to spend approximately fifty percent of your time gossiping about everyone else, so I guess word got out about us.

Before the rest of us could even sign off on it, Becca grabbed the phone and said, "We're your girls, Miss Worthington."

Judging by how pale Alexandra Worthington just got behind her tan, it kind of seems like the "girls" part might not have computed.

She takes a tiny step backward. Her head gives a tiny shake back and forth. "No. No, no. No. No. You're . . ." There's a long pause before she says, "CHILDREN!"

Um, ouch? We're going into *seventh* grade. We're not *that* young!

Becca, Lauren, and Vi can tell something is wrong and they all get up and race over.

"Excuse me, is everything okay?" Lauren asks.

"Everything is most certainly *not* okay," Alexandra Worthington says. I know I should probably call her Miss Worthington or just Alexandra (though not to her face, of course!) but she's just such an "Alexandra Worthington" that I can't.

"I already fired my wedding planner." Alexandra Worthington is getting screechy now. "I can't go crawling back to her. I won't. That's not how I operate."

Oh yeah. If you're waiting for the other shoe to drop, here you go: the wedding planner Alexandra Worthington fired?

That would be Lorelei Pleffer. A.k.a. my mom.

So there's that.

Hence the iron anchor in my belly. Because when Mom finds out her client fired her to hire me, one of us is dead. Me, because Mom has killed me, or Mom, from a broken heart. Either way, things are not looking good for the Pleffer family.

Alexandra Worthington's voice screeches up another note and her hand hits her hip. "Apparently, now I am *sans* planner because *you* are not at all what you represented yourselves to be! Why didn't you *tell* me you were a bunch of kids?"

Other people eating their breakfast are starting to stare at us now and I kind of wish I could melt into the floor. Lance comes out from the kitchen with a crinkled forehead, carrying a tray of biscuits and sausage gravy. Becca, Lauren, and Vi share desperate looks. I would be in on that look too, except at the moment, I'm halfway hoping Alexandra Worthington will turn and walk out before this whole mess goes any farther.

On the one hand, I love my friends and I even love RSVP and I'm still a tiny bit mad at my mom for firing me in the first place and then not making it to any of the parties this summer. If I wanted her attention, *hooo boy*, will this get it. But on the other hand . . . it's my mom we're talking about.

"Pardon me, Alexandra," Becca says. See what I mean? Becca's never afraid of authority figures. She calls her Alexandra to her face. "But we never 'represented' we were adults. In fact, you referenced so many of our clients when you called to hire us, we assumed you knew everything there was to know about us. Why wouldn't we have?"

"Well, none of *them* thought to mention you're barely out of diapers!"

Becca bites her lip, and Lauren claws her fingers into Becca's arm to stop her from answering that comment with whatever she's about to say next. Becca takes a deep breath, smiles oh-so-sweetly at Alexandra Worthington, and says, "Probably they didn't mention our age because how old we are is totes not relevant to how fantastic our party-planning skills are."

Which would have sounded a lot more impressive if Becca had skipped the "totes." Then again, if she had, she wouldn't be Becca.

Alexandra Worthington stares hard at Becca for a second and Becca lifts her chin and stares right back. Neither one blinks. After a couple of seconds, Alexandra Worthington's eyes narrow slightly and she says, "You may have a point."

She takes off her hat, tucks it under her arm, and pushes past us into the restaurant. "Where are we sitting? I'll need to tell you some things about myself if this is to be a successful client/planner relationship. First things first. I do not do liver and chicken steak for breakfast and I sincerely hope none of you do either. If so, I will need to excuse myself because that is just plain disgusting and I won't hear of it."

Okayyyyyyyy, then. I guess we're hired.

Which is a good thing, right?

Right?